Dreamed Awake

A Novel

JEFF CARREIRA

Dreamed Awake
By Jeff Carreira

ISBN-13: 978-1-7357886-2-3

Transdimensional Fiction
P.O. Box 63767
Philadelphia, PA 19147

www.TransdimensionalFiction.com

Cover design by Silvia Rodrigues

Dreamed Awake

A Novel

Jeff Carreira

Transdimensional Fiction
Philadelphia, Pennsylvannia

"Just realize you are dreaming a dream that you call the world and stop looking for ways out...When you have seen the dream as a dream, you have done all that needs to be done."

— Nisargadatta Maharaj

"Dreams pass into the reality of action. From the actions stems the dream again; and this interdependence produces the highest form of living."

— Anaïs Nin

"Whenever someone tells me that they dreamed. I wonder if they realize that they have never done anything but dream."

— Fernando Pessoa

Contents

One: The First Dream of Freddy Peoples. .1

Two: The End of Connie's Life on Madeira Island 9

Three: An Old Nun Bakes Muffins in a Church Tower. 19

Four: Fernando Pessoa Introduces Vicente Guedes 31

Five: Connie Doesn't Get Thrown Overboard. 41

Six: The Third Mate Has a Visitor. 51

Seven: Jeff and Vicente Arrive Onboard .63

Eight: Jeff's Early Explorations of the Dream Realms 75

Nine: Jeff Sees Constantine's Prayers 87

Ten: Constantine Saves Tio Marco 99

Eleven: Constantine Tells His Secret 111

Twelve: Alexandra's Library 121

Thirteen: Alexandra Explains Everything. 133

Fourteen: The Lady in the Red Dress 145

Fifteen: The Captain and Third Mate Discover Hope 151

Sixteen: Beyond the Wall of Fear 159

Seventeen: H. P. Lovecraft Has Arrived .165

CHAPTER 1

The First Dream of Freddy Peoples

THE FIRST TIME I actually met Fernando Pessoa, or at least so I have been told, was in a dream of course. Where else would you meet with a dead poet?

It is interesting to consider why I am so certain that where we met was a dream. To be honest, I am less certain about that today than I was at the time. At the time, I was entirely certain that we had met in a dream. What made me so certain was mainly the fact that I remembered meeting him first thing upon waking in the morning. Anytime I remember something first thing in the morning just after waking up, I assume it must have come from a dream, but why couldn't it have just been a memory of something that happened, just like things I might remember at midday?

I assumed it was a dream, first of all, because I remembered it upon waking in the morning, but second of all, because I was only about four years old in the dream, and when I woke up, I was fifty-six. Of course, I have other memories from when I was four years old that I don't assume are dreams. I assume those are just memories from the past when I was a child. The more I have thought about it, the more difficult I find it to justify calling anything a dream, if by dream we mean something that is less real than something else called reality. That was a big part of Fernando Pessoa's entire point. Everything is a dream to him. Some dreams feel different than other dreams. Some dreams connect with each other in long strings. Some dreams share characters. But they are all dreams.

When I first met him, I didn't know yet that Fernando Pessoa was a master of the dream realms. I was only four years old, so I wouldn't have been able to understand what that meant even if I had. And Pessoa was not just any dream master; he was a master of the entire dreamscape. The dreamscape is the collection of all dreams ever dreamed, and it is where all new dreams are stored forever. It is the marvelous multidimensional space in which all dreams exist.

Pessoa, I eventually learned, is known by some as the master of the thousand and one dreams. The title's reference to the number a thousand and one evidently came from some long-ago era where one thousand was about the highest number anyone could imagine, and so one thousand and one essentially meant infinity. Inaccurate though it may be, the title resonates with a sense of magic and mystery borrowed from the book *One Thousand and One Arabian Nights*, and so it has managed to stick.

None of this I knew that first night.

Look, that's me sitting up in bed. It's very dark, but my little nightlight illuminates the room. The small boy, who is me, is looking around. He can sense something that he cannot see. He seems unusually calm under the circumstances, but his wide eyes betray the fear that is running through him. On the other side of the room is a second bed and his... ah, my brother Steve is still asleep. Don't worry, Steve will not wake up.

In front of the window near my bed is a little red desk. It has iron legs with holes in the feet where it used to be screwed to the floor of an elementary school in town. My parents had bought it when the school closed and then painted it for me. The desktop is hinged in the back, so it lifts up to reveal the space where I keep my writing and drawing projects. I am always writing and drawing. Tomorrow morning, I will write all about the encounter that is about to take place.

There he is. See him? He is barely visible in the corner. Watch as he slowly appears passing through translucency from the invisible realm of dreams to physical manifestation. He is wearing his dark gray, wide brimmed hat, tilted slightly to the right. His small but well-manicured mustache sits below the nose that serves as a resting place for his round spectacles. As was his custom, he wears a long, dark coat. Today he is wearing a white shirt and dark pants with shiny, black leather shoes. He moves very slowly into the room, pulls the small chair away from the red desk, and turns it toward the boy. He sits. The chair was made for a child and so his knees are nearly as high as his neck. He doesn't seem to mind.

"Boa noite, Jeffrey. Tu tens medo de me?" he said, and then, seeing the blank look on the boy's face, he spoke again in English. "Hello, Jeffrey. Are you afraid of me?" The boy's face brightened at hearing words he could understand.

"No. I'm not afraid," the boy said, although he looked terrified.

"That is good, because I am here only to help you. I am here because your great-grandfather sent me."

"Voovoo sent you," the boy said. "Is Voovoo here?" he asked hopefully.

"No, my child, your Voovoo is not here. It is only me tonight."

"Why are you here so late at night? Why didn't Voovoo bring you to see me in the morning?"

"I can only see you at night because I visit you in your dreams. Someday, when I am done teaching you, we will be able to dream together while you are awake during the day, but for now I must see you only at night while you are asleep." Fernando Pessoa was beginning to look uncomfortable sitting on the small chair. He shifted his position to find better balance and then continued. "You see, you are actually asleep now. This," he said making a sweeping gesture with his hand, "is all a dream."

"I'm dreaming right now?" the boy asked. Then he pinched himself on the arm.

"That doesn't work," said Pessoa. "You can't pinch yourself to wake up in a dream. If you pinch yourself in a dream, you will only feel pain. Someday, I will show you that it is possible to pinch yourself in a dream so that you will find a bruise in that same spot on your body when you wake up. That is because your dreams will have become so close to reality that the effects of them carry over into your waking life."

"Why would I want to hurt myself in a dream if I was going to feel it when I woke up?"

"You wouldn't, except to prove that you could."

"Why did Voovoo send you to my dreams?" the boy asked.

"I knew your Voovoo many years ago." Then he added, "Your Voovoo's name is Constantine, Constantine Andrade. Did you know that?"

The boy shook his head no and looked like he had failed an important test, but Pessoa didn't seem to even notice.

"I knew your Voovoo as Connie. We were both teenagers, a little older than you are now. We met on a ship heading for South Africa where we lived together for two years. I was living with my mother, Maria, and my stepfather, Joao. Your great-grandfather started working for my stepfather after we arrived, and for two years, he lived with us. We, your great-grandfather and I, shared a bedroom, just like you and Steve do now." Saying this, Pessoa glanced over at the younger brother still sleeping on the other side of the room. "Did Voovoo ever mention me to you?"

"No, but I can't understand Voovoo very well, so maybe he did, and I didn't know."

"Perhaps," Pessoa said thoughtfully. "I spoke with your great-grandfather recently, and he asked me to come see you. I came as soon as I could."

"Where do you live?" asked the boy.

"I don't live anywhere anymore. You see, I'm actually not alive anymore. I have not been alive for many years. I knew your great-grandfather when we were both teenagers, but I only lived another thirty years more, and your great-grandfather is almost ninety, so he's outlasted me by forty years and he's still here."

"If you're not alive, how did you see Voovoo recently?" the boy asked.

"The same way I am seeing you now. In his dreams. Your Voovoo and I have stayed in contact all these years through our dreams. When we lived together in Durban, that's the city where we lived in South Africa, we developed our dreamwork together." Fernando stopped for a moment to look at the boy's face. "How old are you, boy?" he asked.

"I am almost eight," the boy said with confidence.

"Do you understand what I am telling you?"

"You knew my great-grandfather in Africa when you were both boys, and you learned how to fly into dreams together," the boy said as if he could be expected to receive a good grade for his answer.

"Yes, that is a very good summary."

"Why did Voovoo want you to come see me?" the boy asked.

"Connie," Pessoa started, but then added, "your great-grandfather, had told me soon after you were born that you were a special boy, and that you could fly in and out of dreams like us, but when we spoke last, Connie told me that you had forgotten how to fly into dreams, and he wanted me to visit you to see if I could teach you how again."

"I never knew how to fly into dreams," the boy said.

"It feels like you never knew, but that is only because you don't remember that you did. This is what happens to most people that are born dreamers. For a few years, you move freely between your many dream worlds and this dream that they call the real world. But then, you stop dreaming, or at least you limit your dreaming to just the ones you have at night. You start to live most of the time in the dream called the real world. Then one day, you don't remember there ever were other worlds to live in. You only remember the real world and, every once in a while, a dream you had while you were asleep. The reason you don't think you ever knew how to move through the dream worlds is because you forgot that you did."

The boy was sitting, looking very intently at this strange man with the hat and glasses. He didn't remember ever knowing how to fly in and out of dreams. He just has dreams sometimes. He didn't understand what this man was telling him. He didn't even know who this man was.

"Who are you?" the boy asked. "What's your name?"

"My name is Fernando Pessoa, but why don't you call me Freddy Peoples for now."

"OK, Freddy Peoples. Are you going to teach me how to fly into dreams?"

"Yes, in fact, that is exactly what I am going to do, but not tonight. We have done enough for tonight. You need to get back to sleep. In the morning, if you remember any of this at all, it will all feel like just another dream to you, but that doesn't matter. I will be back very soon on another night, and we will have our first dreaming lesson."

Freddy Peoples stood up and pushed the small chair back under the little red school desk. Then he turned and walked toward the wall. But the boy didn't see a wall. He saw a hole that opened to a dark street. There were lights on the street, but they had candles in them. It was rainy. He was afraid the carpet on his floor was going to get wet and he would get in trouble. When Freddy Peoples was a little way down the street, he turned and waved, very stiffly, back toward the boy. The boy slowly waved in response, then he sat up in bed for about an hour before slowly falling back to sleep.

In the morning, the boy didn't remember anything. He didn't remember Freddy Peoples. He didn't remember any of the strange talk about dreams. And he didn't remember that the strange man with the hat and glasses had promised to return to teach him.

CHAPTER 2

The End of Connie's Life on Madeira Island

AFTER ROWING HIS BOAT down the coast from his tiny village for thirty-five minutes in the hot Madeira sun, it was a relief to step onto the tight cobblestones of the road that leads into the small city of Funchal. Connie, a young boy no more than twelve years old, tied up his small rowboat alongside the many others. He then bent over into the boat and picked out the two buckets full of tomatoes that he had brought to sell. He slung a pole across his shoulders so that the two ends reached outward to his left and his right like an open set of wings. On each end of the pole, he draped the handle of one of the buckets. The pole was heavy on his shoulders, and he would need to maintain his balance or risk losing the tomatoes. The little stones under his feet looked like oversized eggs made of rock and were packed so tightly together that there was hardly any space showing between them. They were hard on his bare feet, but he was used to it by now. Even with the additional load that he was carrying, he walked swiftly along.

The sun was only just rising above the hills, and he had been up long before dawn, as he was every day and had been for the past four years ever since his mother had sent him to live here with his uncle. "It will be better for you to live with Tio Marco," his mother had told him. "Your uncle has a farm, and he will teach you how to be a farmer." The boy had cried during the entire two-day voyage to Madeira.

When he first met his uncle, his uncle looked at him with the stern eyes that he has become so accustomed to. "Stop your bawling," Tio Marco said in a gruff Portuguese dialect. "Perhaps your mother treated you like a child, but here with me you are a man and you will not cry." The boy sniffled and tried to look tough.

As he walked on the road toward the market, he looked down at his feet. They were brown from the sun and the cuffs of his only pair of pants were in tatters. He had come with a small trunk of clothes, but Tio Marco had sold most of them and some had burned in the fire. The fire was not Connie's fault, but he had been blamed for it anyway of course. Everything that upset his uncle was Connie's fault, and almost everything upset Tio Marco.

Now he could hear the sounds of the market; even at this early hour, it was full of sellers and buyers, all wanting to take advantage of the hours before the sun would make it too hot to be out. Mr. Pacheco, the vegetable man, was straightening out the vegetables on his cart.

"Hello, little Connie," said the vegetable man. "What have you got for me today?" Then picking up one of the tomatoes from the left-hand bucket, he continued. "These look very nice and fresh. You're a good farmer; you will live a long and happy life here in Madeira."

Connie looked up at the portly man. There was no expression on the boy's face. He had understood, but as usual, he felt no response to anything he heard. He simply stood and waited for the final pronouncement.

"I will give you five escudos for both buckets."

The boy put the buckets down and held out his hand. He never bargained for a higher price. He didn't know how. His uncle always told him that he had been robbed. Marco would say that any idiot could have easily made twice as much money as Connie did. It was not true. Mr. Pacheco was fond of the boy and always gave him a fair price. Connie, for his part, was fond of Mr. Pacheco and wished that he could live with him instead of Tio Marco.

Mr. Pacheco put five coins in Connie's open hand and then asked, "Have you eaten anything today, boy?"

Connie shook his head no. He was being honest. He had eaten nothing all morning, there was nothing to eat, and he knew better than to eat one of the tomatoes for sale. Mr. Pacheco handed the boy a banana saying, "Eat that and throw the peel in the water on your way back to your uncle's farm. Don't let him see you with it." Mr. Pacheco knew that anything could send Marco into a rage, and he wanted to be sure not to be the cause of trouble for the boy.

Connie nodded his head and said "Obrigado" in his soft and barely audible voice.

Connie took a small leather purse out of his pocket and put the five escudos in it before returning the purse to his pocket. He turned and walked down the cobblestone lane toward the shore where his boat was tied and waiting for him. Once he reached the shore, he untied the boat and pushed it out into the water. Then he jumped in and started rowing the boat up the coast toward his uncle's village. This was his favorite thing in the world. Here in the small boat on the water, his mind finally felt calm. His uncle could not get to him. He had no fears on the water. He was safe. Someday he would simply keep on rowing past his uncle's farm and all the way back to Lisbon where he would find his mother. Or perhaps, he would not stop in Lisbon. Maybe he would row all the way to America where a boy like him could find real work and earn a good living. He knew it would take a long time to row all the way to America, but he liked being on the water so he would not mind.

As he pulled away from the shore, he saw a huge boat way out at sea. It was a big passenger liner with black smoke pouring out of the two stacks that stood on its deck. The stacks leaned backward as if the boat was moving terribly fast and the momentum was blowing them back. The boat was surely headed to the port on the other side of Funchal. Someday, Connie would be brave enough to row the extra distance so that he could see the port for himself, but today he was going to head home.

Three times a week he made this trip to Funchal. On the sea where he felt safe was where he could relax enough to dream. He never dreamt at night. He was too afraid of his uncle to fall soundly asleep. At home, in his small bed he slept each night with one eye open as the saying goes. Out on the water, in his boat, his mind was free to wander. He could be anywhere and do anything. He would sit in the boat and row slowly up the coast, not giving a thought to the rowing. The movement of his body would go on automatically, allowing his mind, heart, and soul to fly freely to other places and times. Today, he was on board that ship way out at sea. He was walking the decks at night. Everyone onboard is asleep, and the decks are empty. There is no moon, but the stars are dancing together everywhere overhead. It is a beautiful night, and the air on the deck is cool and breezy. It is safe to be outside now while everyone is asleep, but by morning he must find a good hiding place.

Connie walks to the edge of the deck and looks out over the water. The small boat, belonging to his uncle, that had brought him up to the rigging on the side of the ocean liner was floating away; soon it would be out of sight. As he stood on his tiptoes looking over the edge of the deck watching the boat drift away, he realized something. This was not a dream. He was on the ocean liner. This was the ship he had seen earlier on his way back from Funchal. Slowly, he remembered arriving back at the shore of Tio Marco's farm. He remembered walking up the path to the small house. He walked past the small building, the one that used to be an outhouse but was now his bedroom. He walked into Tio Marco's house. His uncle was up and drinking from his last bottle of brandy. Connie knew that drinking this early was always bad.

"Come here, boy!" Tio Marco shouted. Connie approached the big man cautiously, holding his hand out in front of him with the small money pouch in his open palm. Marco grabbed the pouch and opened it, spilling the five coins it contained on the table.

"Five escudos!" Marco shouted angrily. "All you got for two buckets of tomatoes was five escudos?" Then he looked at the boy with a look of burning suspicion. "Where is the rest of it, boy! You must have gotten more than this. Give me the rest!"

"That is it," said the boy. "That is what Mr. Pacheco gave me, and he said it was a fair price."

"Never trust Pacheco. He is a crook. How many times have I told you, that man cheats me!"

Connie never saw Marco's open palm swinging toward his head. He only felt the brutal sting of the slap on the left side of his face. His left ear popped, and he heard a loud ringing. His hearing in that ear would be poor for the rest of his life. He fell to the ground and then got up and ran out the door as fast as he could into his tiny room. It was late afternoon. He knew his uncle would not come out of the house on a day when he started drinking so early. He was safe for now. He sat on the small bed stuffed with straw. He had made the bed, and even after three years, it still smelled like an old cow. He sat and he started to feel confused. He was rocking gently up and down as if he was on the sea.

He was on the sea. He was in the boat now again. He still had the purse in his pocket, and he would soon be home. He had been dreaming, but these were his special dreams, not the ones that come and go, but the ones that tell him about things to come. These were dreams about the future. He knew now that when he got home, he would get a bang on his head, and he would sleep terrified again in his little outhouse. He stopped rowing. He was not going to go back this time. He was done with this life. He did not want to live in fear. He did not want to go back to the farm and work every hour of the day for his terrible uncle. This was not the life he wanted. He wanted to go to America. Perhaps that ocean liner, the one way out at sea, was going to America. Most of the big boats were coming from America. He would wait, and he would sneak on that big boat, and he would go and live in America where he could find work and earn money.

He sat in his little boat and noticed that his left ear was ringing. He reached his hand up to his ear, and he felt the dried blood on his earlobe and the side of his neck. How had he been hurt? He had only dreamed of going home. He reached into his pocket and looked into the little leather purse. The five escudos were still there. He had not gone home, because if he had, he would not have this money in his pocket. He reached up to his left ear again. The dried blood was still there. He still heard the ringing from the blow. How could getting hit in a dream make his real ear bleed? He reached his hand over the side of the little boat and scooped up some saltwater in his palm. He used the water to clean the blood from his ear and neck. The cut on his ear stung from the salt. It was a real wound even if he had received it only in a dream.

The boy had a plan; he would wait until dark, and then he would climb up the rigging onto the deck of that ocean liner. He would find a place to hide and only come out when the ship had reached America. But for that, he would need food. He thought about spending his escudos in the market, but if people saw him there, they would know that he had not gone back to his uncle. Someone would tell his uncle, or worse, they would grab him and bring him to his uncle. He could not go back to the market. Instead, he looked for a small farm just outside of Funchal. He slowly rowed his boat to the shore out of sight from the farm and tied it up. It was easy to walk up to the farm, enter the fields, and pick some ripe tomatoes and passion fruit that were growing there. He even found a small sack to put the fruit in. No one would ever notice that it was missing.

His small boat approached the rigging that hung down the side of the ship. It was dark. He was silent as he reached for the rope. The rope was wet and cold. As his fingers touched it, he remembered that this had happened in his dream earlier when he was dreaming awake on the little boat. This exact moment when he reached out his hand and felt the cold wet rope. This moment as he heard the rope slapping up against the sideboards of the ocean liner with each wave. He had lived this moment before in his dream. This very afternoon, while his body sat and rowed unconsciously toward home, he had visited this exact moment and lived through it. Now he was here again. He knew that the climb would be easy, but he would slip once and lose three of his tomatoes to the sea. He started his climb upward. It was easy. When he was nearly to the top, he stopped. This was the moment when he slipped and lost three tomatoes. Maybe he would not have to lose them if he was careful. Since he had seen this moment before and knew what was going to happen, maybe he could change it.

Connie very carefully placed his foot in the rigging, testing it to be sure it was secure, and then slowly lifted himself up. Once he was stable, he secured his other foot higher in the rigging and stepped upward again. He moved slowly and carefully all the way to the top of the railing of the deck. Then he placed his little sack over the side and let it down slowly onto the deck. He swung his feet over the side of the railing and climbed over until he was standing on the deck. He looked back over the edge and saw his little boat floating away. He remembered this exact moment too. Maybe not exact, but very close. Actually, not exact, because now he had all of his tomatoes, and in the dream, he had lost three when he slipped in the rigging. So, the future that he dreamed did not have to happen exactly as it appeared in the dream. The futures that he saw could be changed.

The boy was very tired now. He looked around for a place to hide. There were lifeboats on the deck, and they were covered with heavy cloth. That is where he could hide. It would be hot and dark in the daytime, but he would not be seen there. He walked over to one of the lifeboats and lifted a corner of the cloth. He climbed in. This rowboat was much bigger than the little one he used to go to Funchal, so it would be better for sleeping in, but the floor of the boat was wet. Connie laid down on this back and let himself get wet. Tomorrow, he thought, when it was hot, he would be happy for the water to cool him. As he closed his eyes to fall asleep, he realized that he felt safe. He felt better here, a hideaway on a strange ship, than he ever had with Tio Marco. He might even dream at night tonight.

As Connie began to fall asleep, three beautiful tomatoes sat on the deck of the boat. Somehow, they had managed to fall out of the bag as he was scrambling into the lifeboat. They just sat there waiting. An hour or so after Connie had fallen fast asleep, a large wave made the ocean liner lurch upward. A number of passengers would comment in the morning that the wave had woken them up from a sound sleep. They thought it was very strange that such a large wave would emerge out of what otherwise was a very calm sea. It was as if the wave had been summoned out of the ocean depths just to rock the boat, they said. When the big wave hit the boat, the deck tilted. When the deck tilted, the three beautiful tomatoes rolled across the deck, over the edge, and into the sea. They bobbed up and down as they floated away in the same general direction as the boat had.

Connie never missed the tomatoes, and so he never realized that the integrity of the future had been maintained.

CHAPTER 3

An Old Nun Bakes Muffins in a Church Tower

I DISCOVERED LUCID DREAMING in a book. It was a book called, appropriately enough, *Exploring the World of Lucid Dreaming* by Stephen LaBerge and Howard Rheingold. I found the book in my local, new age bookstore. Stores like that were popular at the time. I lived outside of Boston, and there were two near me. Unicorn Books in Arlington, and Seven Stars in Harvard Square. I found this particular book at the Arlington shop. It was sitting on a display table with a dozen other books on dreams and dreaming.

I was instantly attracted to the cover, and on the back lucid dreaming was defined as the act of becoming consciously aware during the dream state. It claimed that this was an exhilarating experience in which you could enter worlds of your own creation. In these new worlds, you can do the impossible and consciously influence the outcome of your dreams. I was totally hooked. I read the book and practiced the techniques. Soon, I had read other books on lucid dreaming, among them were four of the books by Carlos Castaneda in his series about his apprenticeship with the Yaqui Indian sorcerer, Don Juan Matus from Sonora, Mexico.

All of the books intrigued me, and I practiced all of the techniques that I learned to induce lucid dreams in myself. I kept a dream diary at the side of my bed and religiously wrote any dreams I remembered every morning. I also started to check to see if I was dreaming just about every hour throughout the day. I had an alarm set on my watch to remind me. When it went off, I practiced one of the techniques I had learned that would tell me if I was awake or if I was dreaming. If there was a mirror nearby, I would look into it. I had read that it is impossible to look at yourself in a mirror while you are dreaming, so if you try and cannot look into a mirror, you must be dreaming. The other easy technique is to look for any piece of written material, a book, a magazine, or anything else that has words printed on it. You read the words of any page then turn your head away from the page and, in a dream, the words will always be different when you look back. A related technique involved looking at a clock. Just like with other written material, a dream clock will never read the same time again once you look away from it.

Exploring the World of Lucid Dreaming became my bible. I read and reread it often. It was clear and concise and full of practical techniques. Of course, like millions of other people, I loved the Carlos Castaneda books because, although dreaming figured prominently in Don Juan's spiritual teachings, the books were about much more than that.

They were about spiritual power and other dimensions of reality. They were also about the mysterious relationship of spiritual apprenticeship with a master teacher. All of these things would figure prominently in my life.

Much later in my life, when I was working for a spiritual magazine, I tried to get an interview with Carlos Castaneda. I was the marketing director for our magazine, so I would go to publishing trade shows. Over a few years, I developed relationships with many of my fellow spiritual publishers. Among these relationships was one with the marketing staff that worked for Carlos Castaneda. Generally, there were three women working the booth. They all had short, cropped hair styles. They were all very attractive, and they were all a bit intimidating. One, with blonde hair, seemed to be the senior member of the team. Her name was Susan, and I asked her about the possibility of securing a phone interview with Carlos. Carlos was notorious for not doing interviews and even more notorious for not allowing anyone to take his photograph. For many years, the one public photograph of him had been taken for *Time* magazine. It was a portrait of his face, but with his open hand covering it. You could only see one eye peeking out from between his outstretched fingers.

Castaneda was a master of mystery, and I wanted to talk to him. It was that sense of mystery that had brought him so many readers. My friend Rod had told me that when he was traveling through India as a spiritual seeker in the nineteen-seventies, you could always find Castaneda's books at any little bookshop. Sitting on the shelf among all the Hindu spiritual books, there would always be a copy of

The Teachings of Don Juan, *A Separate Reality*, or *Journey to Ixtlan*.

Susan told me that an interview might be possible, and I asked her if she could arrange it. She said yes, she would try, but she didn't know when. Then she explained, "You see, I can't call Carlos. He doesn't have a phone. I never know where he is. We have an office in Los Angeles, and every two or three months he shows up, unannounced, to check on things. The next time he comes in, I will set it up. Here," she handed me a card, "that's my number. You can call me in a few weeks to remind me."

I took the card and thanked her. I was very excited. Because all the book trade shows happen around the same time each spring, I saw her again the very next month. She said hello when I walked up to her, without smiling of course, and before I had a chance to ask, she said, "He hasn't come yet."

I called her a few weeks later. She still hadn't seen him. I waited another month and called again. "Carlos is dead." Susan said when I asked about the interview. "He died a few months ago, it seems. No one told us. He might have been dead when we first spoke about doing an interview for all I know." She sounded, not upset exactly, but definitely unsettled.

Deception and mystery were such an important part of Castaneda's work and persona. His critics claimed, almost from the start, that there never had been a Don Juan, and that the entire story was a work of fiction. Deception and mystery are powerful tools. Leaving people uncertain about what is true is more powerful than convincing them that you are right. If you convince someone of something, they stop thinking, but if you make them wonder, their mind opens to unknown possibilities. This is what happened to me while studying and practicing lucid dreaming. I opened to the fact that I didn't have the faintest idea what reality was.

I had studied physics as an undergraduate and had been thoroughly convinced by the materialist worldview. The universe was an expanse of three-dimensional empty space filled with solid things made up of atoms. Plain and simple. This scientific worldview was distinctly at odds with the Roman Catholic roots of my childhood. In my second-generation Portuguese American family, I had been captivated by the story of Jesus and the life of the immaterial soul. I had wanted to be a priest until I was told that they only did it for the money. You see, as a child, when I confided in my grandfather my desire to enter the priesthood one day, he said things that implied that priests were fakes who pretended to love Jesus just to make money. When I was older, I realized that his comment probably said more about his relationship to Jesus than anyone else's, but it was enough to turn me away from the church and onto the path that led me straight into the open arms of scientific materialism. I stopped wanting to be a priest and decided that I would be a scientist.

Perhaps my spiritual heart and my scientific mind had both found a home in the study and practice of lucid dreaming. After all, on the back cover of LaBerge and Rheingold's book it talked about a scientifically researched framework for using lucid dreaming.

My first lucid dreaming experience was spectacular. I was having a zombie dream. These were common for me.

And the zombies in my dreams were not the 1960's George A. Romero *Night of the Living Dead* kind that walk slowly and are easily outrun. My zombie dreams feature the Danny Boyle, super-fast kind that swarm you like bees. In the dream, I was running from hundreds, maybe thousands of zombies. They were getting closer and would soon overtake me. At the last possible moment, I saw an old barn in an open field ahead. I had just enough time to reach it and scramble up the drainpipe to the roof before I was caught by the undead horde. Once perched atop the roof, I stopped and looked around. There was a sea of zombies stretched out in every direction. I suddenly realized that I was trapped. The zombies started piling up on all sides of the building, and they were climbing on top of each other to get onto the roof. I was doomed.

But then, a strange thought struck me. "There aren't any real zombies. I must be dreaming."

Suddenly everything changed. I was dreaming! I was dreaming, but I had become awake in the dream. I was conscious of the fact that I was dreaming, while I was dreaming. It was the most exhilarating experience I had ever had up until that point.

But the zombies were starting to crest the edges of the roof, and I needed to act. I had often had dreams where I could fly, and since this was a dream, I reasoned, I can just fly away. In my dreams, the way I fly is by diving off of something tall and careening toward the ground head-first. At the last moment, I arch my back upward, and my whole body swoops up into the air. Eventually I start falling downward again, and I have to repeat the process. By about the third swoop, I am fully airborne.

I ran and jumped off of the peak of the barn. I was heading straight into the outstretched arms of the wildly moaning zombies who were eagerly anticipating the taste of my flesh, but just as they were about to grab me, I arched my back and swooped upward. I felt zombie fingertips graze my belly as I flew over them. Two more swoops and I was fully airborne high up in the sky, and the zombies were far behind me and out of sight. Once I was out of danger, my heart started pounding, not from the terror of zombies, but with the excitement of realizing that I was dreaming, and I could go anywhere I wanted. For reasons I do not understand, I felt very compelled, arbitrarily it seemed to me, to fly to France.

I flew all night over the Atlantic Ocean. I was above the clouds, and the moon was full and bright in a dark blue and purple sky that sparkled with the light of a blanket of stars. The wind at this high altitude blew right through me. It was cool but comfortable, and below me through breaks in the clouds, I could see shimmering ripples on the water's surface. It was one of the most beautiful experiences I've ever had. I felt so alone and so free. I honestly didn't want that trip to ever come to an end.

Hours later, as the sun began to come up and all the clouds below me cleared, I could see farmland stretching all around me on the ground. As far as I could see there were fields upon fields spreading out in every direction. Way off in the distance I saw buildings. I knew that it was Paris, but I didn't know exactly when. The shape of the buildings that I could see convinced me that it was not the present that I lived in. As I flew closer to the old buildings, I saw a tall steeple in what appeared to be a church or monastery. It

JEFF CARREIRA

was still dusk, and I could see a light in the highest window in the steeple tower. I flew straight into the open window and perched myself on the stone sill. Outside was a city that looked like it came out of the Arthurian legends or perhaps a Dickens novel. Inside the window, I saw a small kitchen with a stove made of iron. I could smell something sweet, like cookies baking. I sat on the windowsill. I was at least 200 feet above the street below, but I wasn't afraid.

I stopped and relaxed. I was dreaming. Everything around me was a dream. It was all constructed by the imaginative power of my mind. And it was all magnificently real. The dim light shining on the horizon, the dancing glow of the fire in the stove that flickered through the open slats in the door of the iron stove, the musty damp smell of the air, it was all so real! I noticed some wetness on the windowsill near my foot. I reached down and touched it with my finger. It felt wet. It felt just like real water. I rubbed the water between my fingers and held them close to my eyes. It looked just like real water. I touched my fingers to my lips. No difference. There was no way to tell that this was not real water. There was no way to know that this water was being produced by my own mind. It felt utterly real.

This was the first time it struck me that there is nothing inherently dreamlike about a dream while you are in it. Inside the dream, it all seems real. Even fanciful and preposterous aspects of dreams feel natural and obvious in the context of the dream. Dreams only feel like dreams in comparison to our experience, or memory, of real life. For instance, this felt like a dream at the time mainly because I knew that I couldn't fly in real life. I knew that in real life, I didn't live in this time period, but if I were to forget my real life, then this would be the only life I knew, and it would feel totally real. If I forgot my real life, this dream would become my real life. You see, dreams, however bizarre they might seem in relation to our real life, are the only reality there is when you are in them.

Over time, as I had more and more lucid dreams and explored the enhanced capacities I had as a dream traveler, I would never be able to get over this. There is nothing inherently dreamlike about a dream from the inside of it. And of course, I couldn't avoid getting mired in the question of what made my real life different from any other dream. Yes, it felt totally real from inside, but so did any dream when I was in it. The main thing that made my real life feel real was the fact that I remembered so much of it. When I enter a dream, I generally don't have a memory of the entire life I have in that dream. I usually just pop into the middle of a life already in progress. I have knowledge of the moment in which I appear, and perhaps a vague sense of the life I was in the middle of, but no detailed memories of the past. What if I dreamed the same dream over and over again? What if I remembered more and more from the same dream life? At what point would that dream start to feel more real than others? At what point would that dream start to feel as real as my real life? At what point would it feel more real? These were the questions that drove me to want to explore the worlds that opened up in my lucid dream experiences. I wanted to keep entering new dream-worlds so I could explore them from the inside.

As I sat on the stone windowsill, I heard footsteps that sounded as if they were climbing stone steps. Then the large wooden door opened with a loud moan. An old woman dressed in a nun's habit walked into the room. She walked, slightly stooped over forward, towards the stove. As she reached the stove, she stopped for a moment and slowly turned toward me.

"Hello there," she said calmly as if finding a man perched on her high tower windowsill was a common occurrence for her. "Do you like muffins?"

"Yes, I like muffins," I answered.

"You must be a flyer," she said, "because you don't look like someone that just scaled a wall. Your hair looks like you just flew across the sea. Are you a flyer?"

"Yes, I guess I am."

"Where did you come from?"

"I'm dreaming. I was dreaming that I was being chased, and I started flying to escape, and then I decided to come here," I said. "Do you know that this is all a dream?" I asked.

"Actually, right now, this is two dreams, yours and mine. In my dream, I am a sixteenth century holy woman who came up to get her muffins… oh no, the muffins!" She turned abruptly and opened the oven door with a stick. Then, using an old cloth to protect her fingers, she picked out a pan filled with freshly baked muffins. Everything I could see looked old, except the muffin pan, which looked like I could have purchased it yesterday… in my waking life yesterday, that is.

"Good, they didn't burn." She continued, "Now where was I… oh yes, in my dream I am a sixteenth century holy woman who is getting her muffins out of the oven and noticing a strange man sitting on her windowsill. Since discovering this man doesn't seem to frighten me, I assume it has happened many times. Your dream involves escaping from zombies and realizing you are dreaming. You see? There are two dreams intersecting here."

She looked at me, and I looked at her. This was the first other person I had ever actually met and talked to in a lucid dream. I didn't even bother to wonder how she knew about the zombies. Instead, the question that captured my mind was where were her words coming from? They must be coming from the same mind that was producing the words that I was thinking now. How come I didn't know what she was going to say before she said it, since it was all coming from my mind? I sat and looked at her.

"Dreams are not just happening in your mind," she said as if she heard my thoughts. "The dreamscape is a shared space of dreaming. Dreams overlap and interweave. Most of the time, you are simply living out your own dream. In that simple case, everything in the dream belongs to you. It is all a creation of your imagination. Of course, even in that case, most of it is being created from unconscious parts of your mind, so it feels completely independent of you in the dream. If I were that kind of dream character, you still wouldn't know what I was going to say before I said it, because my words would be coming from your unconscious. But I am not that kind of character. I am not a character in your dream; I am a dreamer like you are. I am a much more experienced dreamer than you, so I know that I am a dreamer and I can recognize you as one right away. I wouldn't bother having this conversation with you if you were just an image from my unconscious, what little there is left of that in me."

She stopped and looked at me oddly. "Oh, look what I've gone and done. Your brain is getting overwhelmed with all of this. You feel that buzzing in your body, the tingling in your nervous system."

"Yes," I said. "It feels like nervous energy. I understand what you are saying, but I can't believe it. You are another dreamer. I am in your dream, and you are in mine. How do I know this isn't just a regular old dream and everything that you are saying is a projection from my unconscious mind?"

"You don't, of course, but that is not the point. I've given you too much information all at once, and I woke up your analytical mind. It is now chewing on everything you just heard, trying to figure it all out. Once your analytical mind wakes up and gets busy, all the effort and excitement will soon wake up your body and pull you out of the dream. You're about to wake up. I can see your eyes glazing over. Come back when you can."

…

I woke up in my bed. What a wonderful dream. I had been lucid, truly lucid in the dream. I was talking to a nun and smelling muffins. I could hardly wait until I could go back to sleep to see if I could wake up in my dreams again and go visit the old nun again.

CHAPTER 4

Fernando Pessoa Introduces Vicente Guedes

THE FIRST TIME I remember meeting Fernando Pessoa was, according to him, not the first time we had met. It seems that nearly twenty years earlier we had met the first time in a dream. I had no memory of that first meeting, but Pessoa assured me that not only had we met that initial time many years ago, but we've continued to meet regularly since then. Until tonight, we had always met in dreams that I didn't remember in the morning. This time would be different, he said. This time I would remember because now I was ready to remember.

This meeting, the one I was going to remember, started when I woke up in the middle of the night and saw an odd man standing in the corner of my bedroom. He wore a long, dark coat and a wide brimmed hat tilted to the right. He had round glasses with wire frames. He just stood there. I was strangely unafraid of him. It felt totally normal to have this odd man in my bedroom. I looked over and saw my wife, Roxy, asleep next to me in bed.

"You are a lucid dreamer," the man asked me.

"Yes. I've had lucid dreams," I answered.

"That wasn't a question. I know you are a lucid dreamer. I am the one who has been teaching you how to do that."

"No. I've been learning about it from books," I said.

"Do you think those books could give you the skill you now have? Of course, because of our work you were drawn to such books, but believe me, you found nothing of value in any of them that I hadn't already told you."

"I haven't even met you before," I said, and then I asked, "Who are you anyway?" I cocked my head to the right and then slowly again to the left. "Who are you and why are you here? Am I dreaming? Is this a dream? Yes, this must be a dream. I'm lucid right now, aren't I?"

"Yes, this is a dream, but not quite the kind you are thinking of. You are lucid but you are also dreaming right now. You are dreaming that you are waking up in a dream, which is different than actually waking up in a dream. You are dreaming that you are awake. In the morning, you will find yourself very confused. On the one hand, it will feel like you had a lucid dream, and yet it will also feel like you just woke up from a dream about being lucid. I have been working with you for years. Not every night, but many nights. I have been teaching you the art of dreaming." The man with the hat paused for a moment before continuing. "I am sorry, you asked who I am. I am Fernando Pessoa. I was, and still am, the greatest poet of Portugal. Have you heard of me?"

"Yes. I've heard of you. Mr. Silva, my Portuguese teacher in high school, taught us about you and your poems. He was particularly fond of *The Book of Disquiet*. I liked your writing. I even bought a copy of your book, but I haven't read much of it."

"Yes, yes, I know. I, ah, encouraged you to buy the book, but I didn't seem to be able to inspire you to read it," Pessoa said, seeming a little hurt.

"So, you are Fernando Pessoa," I said changing the subject. "And now that you say it, I can see that you are. I recognize you from your photos. And you say that this is a dream, but not a lucid dream, because I am only dreaming that I am lucid and so I am not truly awake." Then I added, "By the way, my name is Jeff."

"Yes, I know who you are, Mr. Carreira. We have been meeting for years, and even though you remember none of it, I remember it all. And regarding what you said about this dream, you are completely correct. And I am here to continue your education in the art of dreaming. When we first met many years ago, I explained to you what we were doing together, but you were too young to understand, so now that I am in a dream that you will actually remember, I will explain again. To start with, I am here at the request of your great-grandfather Constantine."

"Voovoo? But Voovoo's been dead for almost ten years."

"Yes, and he outlived me by over fifty. Nevertheless, he is the reason I am here to teach you about dreaming. And now that you are sufficiently adept in the craft of lucid dreaming, I understand better why Connie wanted it to be you."

"Wanted what to be me?" I demanded.

"Sorry, we will go into all that soon enough. Let us say for now that Connie needs your help."

"But I already told you, Connie is dead. He died ten years ago."

"Only his body is dead. A master dreamer like Connie will live forever in the dream realm. So, in a sense, Connie doesn't really need your help, you do. You need your own help."

"Why do I need to help myself?"

"We are wasting too much time on this. We have an appointment, and I don't want to miss it. So, this will be the last word on this topic for now. Connie was a master dreamer like me. He realized himself completely into the dreamworld. Nothing that would happen to his body would touch him in the dream world because he had given up all attachment to the body. He was free. He had attained enlightenment. But you, you are very much attached to your physical existence, and even though you are destined to be a dream master, you are not one yet. And someone, and I don't know who yet, is trying to stop you from attaining mastery and perhaps trying to erase Connie's mastery too. They are trying to alter Connie's life so that he never becomes a dream master and you are never even born. So, you see, by helping Connie's life stay on track, you not only help Connie, but you ensure that you are here."

I just looked at him. I was beginning to feel anxious about all this.

"It is too soon for all this. It doesn't matter right now. What matters now is that you attain the third and fourth stages of dream mastery. Tonight, I want to introduce you to someone, a friend of mine; his name is Vicente Guedes. Actually, you have met him a few times before, but you will not remember. Like me, he is a master dreamer, and he will be here to help you move into stage three dreaming, which is a bit of a specialty of his. You will soon discover that your dream life has become your real life, and what you have been taught to call your real life is actually a distraction from what is most real. Ultimately, our goal will be to train you in the final stage of dreaming, which is how to dream the inconceivable and make it visible, but that will take time, and to help Connie, you only need to master the first three levels, and you have already mastered the first two."

Pessoa turned away from me saying, "Oh, here is Mr. Guedes now."

Pessoa was looking behind him toward the wall, or at least what used to be a wall. What was there now was a hole that faded at its edges. Through the hole, I could see a beach and, beyond the beach, the ocean. The sunlight shone through the large hole in the wall, and I could smell salt sea air and hear the screeches of seagulls as they circled around fishing boats floating by off in the distance. A man walked toward us through the sand. He was wearing a button-down white shirt with long sleeves, brown pants, and black shoes. He was distinctly not dressed for the beach. He had a short goatee on his chin and a mustache similar to Pessoa's under his nose.

"Hello, Vicente," Fernando said. "Thank you for coming again, my friend. Jeff..." he said looking back at me again. "…this is Vicente. Vicente, you've already met Jeff of course."

"Very nice to meet at a time when the meeting will be remembered," said Vicente.

"Nice to meet you too, although I feel like the odd man out since you two already seem to know me," I replied.

Ignoring my comment, Pessoa went on. "Vicente is the author, rather, the heteronym of the first part of *The Book of Disquiet*, and he wrote extensively on the art of dreaming and the four stages of dream mastery." Pessoa paused and looked back at the man who had just walked in from the beach. "Vicente, I will let you begin."

"The art of dreaming," Vicente began, "is an art unlike any other art because it involves a complete disconnecting of the senses from all of reality. This is not so difficult to attain when the body is asleep because then the senses are also asleep. But in the waking state, when every sense is vibrantly alive, it is nearly impossible to disconnect yourself from the world of sensation that your senses create. The art of dreaming is a perfectly passive art requiring total surrender of all effort. Any attempt to control or direct the outcome of the dream will end the dream. You must surrender fully to a different reality and allow it to be what it is. When you have mastered the art of perfect passivity, it is then possible to learn to, ever so gently, influence what happens in the dream. This is not an act of effortful manipulation of the dream. It simply means surrendering to one possibility and not to others. In this mode of selective surrender, you can gain some degree of influence over the course that the dream takes. You have already mastered the first two stages of the art. You worked diligently for hours each day without knowing what you were actually doing."

"How?" I asked. "How have I been training for years? What have I been doing to train?"

"What is your favorite activity?" Vicente asked.

"Reading," I said.

"And what do you like to read?"

"Novels."

"And what do you love most about reading novels?"

"I love losing myself in the story."

"That is exactly how the work starts. The first level of the work starts by reading novels and losing yourself in them. You want to lose yourself in your novels so deeply that you forget the world around you. Can't you see how reading a novel that way is not very different from dreaming?" Vicente asked.

"Yes. But I wasn't trying to master anything. I just love reading novels," I said.

"You loved reading them because of the work we were doing at night. We didn't allow you to remember the work when you woke up because that just complicates everything. People start to get so caught up in trying to figure out what is going on in their dreams that the work comes to an end. So, we have learned that it is better to keep your waking self in the dark about the work."

"So why are you going to let me remember tomorrow? Won't I get all caught up in trying to figure this very conversation out in the morning?" I said triumphantly.

"If we are successful tonight, you are going to experience a whole new world of possibility, and it will be so captivating that you won't have time to worry about anything else." He paused, then remembering what he had been saying, he went on, "The novels were only the start of the work. We also encouraged you to be interested in spirituality and dreams and meditation and all the things you are engrossed with. Are not all those things also things that you love?"

"Yes," I said. I was beginning to realize that my whole life was not what I had thought it was. The things that I loved, the things that I did, were they all being influenced by Vicente and this dream work?

"Tell me, Jeff. Who is the person you feel closest to?"

"Honestly?" I asked.

"Yes."

"Holden Caulfield from *The Catcher in the Rye*," I answered honestly.

"That is a clear indication of the first level of dream mastery. The characters in novels become more important to you than the real people around you. I have watched you become so absorbed in a book that you have forgotten to eat all day. You have missed appointments. Skipped studying for exams. You even called in sick to work once to finish a novel. Over and over again, you have shown that you are willing to sacrifice your real life for a fictional one, and fictional lives are not very different from dreams." Vicente paused as if to allow me to understand the deeper implications of what he was saying, but what I noticed was Roxy sleeping soundly next to me.

"Why doesn't she wake up?" I asked.

"Do your dreams generally wake her up?" Vicente asked rhetorically. I got it. She wasn't going to wake up because this was a dream, and even if she did wake up, it would only be her dream self that did. Then Vicente continued. "You reached second level mastery a month ago. That is why we are here now."

"What happened a month ago?" I asked.

"Do you remember when you were reading *Zorba the Greek* and you noticed that you had bruises on your arms exactly the way you imagined Zorba might have gotten them in one of the fights in the story?"

"Yes, but I really thought I had bumped my arm without noticing it."

"But that is not what happened. You see, at second level mastery you will physically experience the effects of the action of the story. Your consciousness and your nervous system have become so fused with the story that when something happens to a character in the story, the effects show up on your own body. You have become a conduit through which a story, or a dream, crosses over from the purely mental world of ideas into the physical material world. We had been waiting for a sign like that for a few years now. It is a sign that you are ready to master the third and fourth stages of dreaming."

I started to wonder about something. "Are you telling me that all of this is written in *The Book of Disquiet*?"

"Yes, indeed it is."

"Now I wish I had read it all the way through," I said.

"I am sure you will," said Pessoa. I had actually forgotten that he was in the room. He continued, "But it will not be tonight. Tonight, you need to master, or at least become competent enough to do, level three and four dreaming. Then we have to go and make sure your great-grandfather stays true to his life path and ensure that you are born.

Come on, Vicente, don't drag this out. We need to get going."

CHAPTER 5

Connie Doesn't Get Thrown Overboard

CONNIE'S STOMACH WAS CLUTCHING. He had made it through the night and most of the day before his fruit ran out, but now as he began to feel the darkness of night returning, he was thirsty and hungry. Fifteen hours inside the lifeboat in the hot sun with the heavy canvas covering over it had made him delirious. He tried to sleep, but it was too uncomfortable. He was terrified. What had he done?

He lifted up the edge of the canvas and looked out onto the deck. He could still see five men rushing about. They all spoke in English, and he didn't understand much English. He didn't really care about what they were saying. His attention had been captivated all day by a barrel full of water. It was on the other side of the deck, and it had a ladle attached to it by a rope. He had been watching the sailors drink water from it all day. He was just waiting for the moment when he could climb out of the small boat that he was currently imprisoned in and run over and drink his fill. He just needed to wait until the deck was clear. He closed the canvas cover and lay back down. His eyes fluttered as he hovered somewhere between wakefulness, sleep, and what felt like death.

He must have slept, because when he opened his eyes again, it was pitch dark in his little boat covered by the heavy canvas. He opened the corner of the canvas and could hardly see anything. Slowly and quietly, he lifted the canvas up and slipped out of the boat. He looked around. No one was on the deck. He moved carefully toward the barrel. It was wide open and full of water. Seeing all that water removed all of Connie's caution. He grabbed the ladle and plunged it into the water with a loud splash. Bringing the ladle to his mouth, he gulped down the water. It spilled down his chin and onto the deck. He did it again with no regard for being heard. He was a dry sponge soaking up the liquid. His body had completely taken control of him.

"Who are you?" he heard a voice from behind call out to him. He froze. He was caught. He was a stowaway caught on the deck stealing water. He suddenly felt the full panic of realizing that he didn't belong here. Would they throw him overboard? An image of himself floating in the ocean watching this ship move farther and farther away emerged in his mind. He turned to see a boy of about his own age. "Well? Who are you? What's your name?" Connie knew enough English to understand the question.

"My name is Constantine, but you can call me Connie," he said.

The new boy replied in Portuguese this time, "My name is Fernando, Fernando Pessoa, and you can call me

Fernando, or Pessoa. You are Portuguese, but I can hear in your voice that you are not from Lisbon?"

"I was born in Lisbon, but my mother sent me to live with my uncle in Madeira Island. I think I sound like an islander now."

"You do," Fernando said with unmasked disdain. "What are you doing on this ship? Are you here with your mother too?"

"No, I climbed onto this ship and then hid in that boat all day," Connie said pointing to the little lifeboat that had become his home. For some reason, he had no fear of telling Fernando the truth.

"That sounds awful. Why did you do that?"

"My uncle, Tio Marco, is a wicked man. He made me work all day. He didn't let me go to school. And he beat me. I didn't want to live with him anymore, so I ran away onto this ship. I want to go to America and find good work there," Connie answered.

"But this boat is not going to America."

"It is not?" Connie asked pensively. "Where is it going?"

"It is going to Africa. That is where I am headed with my mother. Her new husband, my stepfather, is waiting for us there. He is an official in the English government. My mother says it will be a good life for us, but I want to be in Lisbon. Lisbon is my home and that is where I want to be, but I would rather be with my mother in South Africa than with my relatives in Lisbon. I guess we are both lost souls in the world." Fernando put his arm over Connie's shoulder in a gesture of comfort and comradery.

Just then, the sound of loud boots walking towards them came from around the corner. "Hurry," whispered

Fernando, "get back in your boat." Connie dashed across the deck like a jackal and scurried into the boat before the sailor emerged into sight.

"What are you doing out here so late, boy?" the soldier asked Fernando.

"I couldn't sleep, so I came out to get some air." Fernando spoke decent English, but with an obvious Portuguese accent.

"Oh, you are the little Portuguese son of Marie. Your mother is a pretty one," the sailor said with a sly smile. Fernando ignored the gesture, and the sailor became rigid fearing that he had said too much. "You should not be out here alone this late," he barked. "Come with me. I am going to take you back to your cabin."

From inside his lifeboat, Connie could hear the loud footsteps of the sailor becoming more distant. He didn't move, he hardly breathed, until he couldn't hear any footsteps. When all was silent, he relaxed. At least he had a belly full of water and a new friend, maybe.

Connie woke in the morning when a loaf of bread and some cheese struck him on his shoulder. He realized in an instant that his new friend, Fernando, had slipped some breakfast into his boat. After eating nothing but fruit for two days, and nothing at all since yesterday afternoon, the bread and cheese tasted like it had been made in heaven. Connie gobbled down the food and then laid back to think.

He didn't know much about Africa and had no interest in living there. All he had ever heard about Africa was that it was full of starving children. It didn't sound any better than life with his uncle. But Fernando was going there with his mother, so maybe it was a good place to live after all.

He wondered what language they spoke in Africa, and he hoped that he could live near Fernando, because at least he was Portuguese. He laid back again and started to doze off.

The next time he was awoken, it was because a hard shoe had hit him in the face. He opened his eyes and saw that Fernando had climbed into the boat with him.

"Hello, Connie," Fernando offered with a smile. "I was very careful to make sure that no one saw me come in." In the daytime sun, it was quite bright under the canvas and very hot. "It is more uncomfortable here than I imagined. How do you survive it?"

"It is awful, but I just try not to think about it."

"What do you do in here all day?" Fernando asked.

"I dream," Connie answered. "Yesterday, I was dreaming of my life in America. I was walking around my daughter's house toward the garden in the back. The house was painted green, and I was living there with one of my daughters and her husband. I was very old, but I had lived a good life. Today, I am dreaming of leaving Africa. I am dreaming of another ship like this one but going to America. I see myself in a cabin with a ticket. I am not hiding in a boat. I am a real passenger."

"Do your dreams ever come true?" Fernando asked.

"Yes, often I dream of things that happen later. Even when I am dreaming on purpose, this sometimes happens, but often it does not also," Connie confessed.

"Sometimes I dream of things that happen later too," said Fernando. "I have never met anyone else who does that. I think we should work together. We should figure out how we do it and get better at it. What do you think?" Fernando said, holding out his hand, intending to shake on

JEFF CARREIRA

it with Connie. But before they had time to shake and seal the arrangement, the canvas covering flew off of the boat.

"Oh, it's you again. Your mother needs to keep a better eye on you." It was the same sailor that took Fernando home last night. Then noticing the other boy, he added, "And who have we here? A stowaway, it seems. Shark food." The sailor grabbed Connie by the ear and pulled him out of the boat. "Get out of there, you little sneak."

Connie screeched slightly, feeling the pain in his ear. It was the same ear that still hurt because he had dreamed that he had gotten struck there by his uncle.

"He is my friend," Fernando cried out. "Let him go. My mother and I will take care of him. You don't really want to have to deal with a stowaway, do you? My mother will pay for his food for the rest of the voyage."

The sailor stopped to think. It just so happened that he was already not in the good graces of the captain because of an incident involving a drunken brawl during their stay in Madeira. He didn't relish being the one presenting this problem for the captain to solve. If the lady would promise to keep the boy out of sight, it would save him a lot of trouble. As for himself, he'd just as soon throw the boy overboard, but that would surely bring a heap of trouble.

"Your mother wants to take care of this vagrant?" the sailor asked suspiciously.

"Yes, I told her about him last night. I told her that I had made a friend and that he had nowhere to sleep. I asked her if he could stay with us. She said yes. That's why I came here today. To get him and bring him to our cabin, but we started talking and then you came. He would have been hidden and out of your hair for the rest of the trip if you hadn't heard us." Connie didn't know if Fernando was lying or telling the truth, but he was happy not to have to be the one explaining what was going on.

"We're going to go straight to your cabin now to see your mother. Then we will find out if she really wants this boy in her cabin. I think you're lying about that, and if you are, there will be hell to pay, and this stowaway will pay it." The sailor pulled Connie by the ear and Fernando by the wrist as he walked away. Connie grimaced as he was tugged along, but soon they were at the door of a first-class cabin. The sailor knocked hard. "Maria. This is J. Edwards, the third mate of this vessel. I found your son and his friend on the deck and brought them back here."

The door opened and Fernando's mother stood in the doorway. She was wearing a black silk dress with a ruffled collar up to her chin. The dress was very pretty, covered in black lace. She also wore a short cape draped over her shoulders. She had shoulder length curly hair that was pulled back in a bun. Her face was as pretty as her dress. She had large brown eyes, a delicate nose, and a broad, open smile. As she listened to the third mate, an expression of fury glanced across her face but was immediately followed by a broad smile.

"Oh, Fernando," Maria said looking down at her son. "Is this your friend Connie? The one you told me about last night?"

"Yes, Mother. I was going to get him today like we agreed."

"Thank you for bringing the boys to me, sir. I assume that you would like me to take care of this boy and be very discrete about it." She held out her hand and placed a few coins in the open hand of the third mate. "That's a little something for your trouble."

The third mate looked confused, but he liked the feeling of the coins in his hand. "Please, ma'am," he said politely, "keep this boy in your cabin until we arrive in Durban. Don't let anyone see him."

"Yes, I certainly will," she said, stepping away from the doorway to clear a path for the boys. "Now you two get in here."

Once the door shut behind her, leaving the third mate in the hallway, she turned to the boys. Fernando and his new friend were standing side by side, both looking down at the floor.

"Now who is going to tell me what this is all about?" Maria demanded. Fernando immediately relayed the whole story from his point of view to his mother. He even told her what he had heard from Connie about his life in Madeira and running away from his uncle. Connie was again relieved to not have to talk. Connie didn't like talking much under any circumstances, but in circumstances like these, even less so.

Maria's face had a stern look as Fernando started the story, but it was soft and open by the end. "So, you are running away from your uncle?" she asked Connie directly.

"Yes, ma'am," Connie said. "Just like Fernando said it."

"Mom," Fernando interrupted using a tone of voice that made it sound like he had something very important, and maybe even shocking, to say. "He's a dreamer, like us."

"Is he now?" Maria said looking down at Connie with real interest. "Is that true? Do your dreams come true?"

"Sometimes they do."

"Who taught you how to dream?" Maria asked.

"No one did. I just started doing it. I thought everyone could."

"Dreaming, the way you dream anyway, is not something everyone does. It is a gift." Maria paused and looked at Fernando. "So, what are we going to do, Fernando? I thought you were talking about an imaginary friend. I didn't realize you had met a real boy."

"Mother, please let him stay with us. He can sleep in my bed with me. It is only a few more weeks, and then we will be in South Africa." Fernando looked up at his mother with his brown eyes wide open. Fernando always had a sad look on his face, but at this moment it was heartbreaking.

"Of course, we are going to keep him with us. What else will we do, toss him overboard?" Maria said definitively. "I hope I will not regret this, young man," she added wagging a long finger in Connie's face.

"You won't, ma'am. You won't. Thank you, ma'am. Thank you." Connie was beside himself.

"So, tell me Connie, did you dream about this?" Maria asked.

"Yes, ma'am. I dreamed exactly this moment last night."

CHAPTER 6

The Third Mate Has a Visitor

J. EDWARDS, THE THIRD mate, woke up in the middle of the night and sat bolt upright. His first name was Jonathan, but he always went by Edwards, or with passengers, J. Edwards. He was just a little closer to sixty than fifty, and this was his first assignment as a third mate. It had been a long road to get a third mate position. He had been a seaman all his life, starting at age thirteen as a cabin boy. He had never done anything else. He was what they call a sea dog. Being the third mate on this ship was a very important step for him. It was late in his career, but if he did well, he might get a permanent post as third mate, and he would be set for life. This was his first third mate posting, and he had almost blown it during the leave on Madeira Island.

The ship was taking on a few passengers, and many of the seamen were granted a twenty-four hour leave to spend in Funchal. Edwards had gone straight to a tavern where the whisky was flowing. He was gruff and liked to drink and fight on his time off. But with his current rank as a third mate, this kind of activity was no longer tolerated, but he hadn't realized that yet. He should have stayed on-board, but he simply didn't know better. So, he drank and spoke loudly. He winked at the pretty Portuguese island girls, and he attracted the disdain of at least one of the young Portuguese men.

"Hey, old man," the Portuguese man… really a boy, said. "You are too loud. Your tone and your crude mouth are offensive to the ladies." The young man glanced back toward four young women who were standing together, and all of them seemed to appreciate that he was looking out for them. The girls all wore skirts that hung below the knee. Their blouses were all various shades of white, and all were decorated with lace. One of the girls was particularly attractive, and Edwards immediately realized that this show of bravado was all about her. The young man was obviously trying to win her affections. He was looking directly at her half of the time that he spoke. Edwards had beat up many men to win a night with a young lady. He would find any excuse to start a brawl, but unlike this young man, Edwards knew enough to pick a fight he could win.

"I think you should move on to the next tavern now, soon you will have drunk all that this place has on hand and leave none for the rest of us." The young man laughed, and the four girls and a couple of other Portuguese men laughed with him. Edwards knew that he could make this young man's night by just taking his leave right then. The young man would then go straight over to the beautiful young woman and ask her if she was alright. She would be fine because nothing had happened, but she would feign that it was upsetting to her and they would walk outside to talk.

Edwards could have made his night right there, but he didn't. Of course, later he wished that he had. It would have been so much easier to have just walked away and gone to the next tavern on the street. But he didn't. "Maybe you should push me out the door," Edwards burst out in his most aggressive voice. Immediately, terror flashed though the young man's eyes. He suddenly realized that he had started something he had no intention, and no ability, to finish. It was the liquor in his belly that had got this going, but now the situation had moved beyond his control.

The young man thought fast. "Perhaps we settle this on the table," he said, looking down at the table and gesturing with his arm that he was challenging Edwards to an arm-wrestling match. An arm-wrestle to decide the outcome struck Edwards as utterly ridiculous. Again, he could have just walked out mumbling something about not wanting to play children's games. He could have saved face for both of them and avoided what was about to happen. He should have done exactly that, but instead, he sat down, banged his elbow on the table, and looked up at the boy.

"The loser buys a round for everyone," Edwards said. The young man had no option but to agree and sit down.

They sat down on opposite sides of the table and grasped hands. Edwards' arm, from wrist to shoulder, was at least twice as thick as the young man's was. There was only one possible outcome to this match. The four women moved closer, but not too close. A small crowd had gathered. Once again, Edwards had the chance to create an easy end to this altercation, and this time, he decided to do just that. He would simply win this match handily and walk out. No more harm done. He would have proven his prowess and defended his honor. The young man would have lost the match, but without too much shame. Simple.

Edwards locked eyes with the young man. In those eyes, he didn't see any fear, only resignation. The young man had no hope of winning and he knew it. It was clear that he wouldn't even really try to win. Edwards tensed up his muscles and one of the young man's male friends started to count backwards from ten to start them off. 10...9...8...

Edwards saw a beautiful woman behind the young man. She stood about ten feet away, but in clear sight. She was wearing a red dress, very tightly fitted over her shapely body. The neck was cut unconventionally low for this island. The cleavage between her large breasts was thrust upwards. Her eyes were dark and perfect. Her lips covered with brilliant red lipstick. She stood with one leg slightly forward and one hip sticking to the side. She looked right into Edwards' eyes. 7...6...5...

As he watched her, she winked at him. He felt an electric bolt of sexual arousal between his legs. He had never experienced anything like this. He had never seen a woman so completely and irresistibly alluring as this. 4...3...2...1

Without knowing what he was doing, Edwards opened his palm so his own fingers would not hit the table and then slammed the young man's hand down on the hard surface so hard that people later claimed they heard the bones of his knuckles break from the other side of the room. The young man screamed loudly and then started to whimper like a baby. The four women stepped back, also screaming. The young man's two friends rushed at Edwards. Punches began to fly. Bodies hit the floor. More seamen joined the fight and then more Portuguese men. People were screaming "Fight!" Others were screaming "Stop!" Edwards saw the woman in the red dress walking out the door. As she passed through the threshold, she looked back through the chaos at Edwards and winked again, nodding her head and inviting him to come with her. Edwards fought his way to the door and walked out. She was nowhere to be seen.

The next morning, Edwards found himself in a holding cell speaking to the captain from behind bars. "What is wrong with you, Edwards?" the captain asked. "I know how important this post is to you, so why would you throw it all away for nothing? You realize I have to fire you now? I have to get rid of you and leave you here. You will forfeit all of your back pay. If you are lucky, you can find work and earn enough money for passage back to England in a few months. And once you get back, you will never find another third mate appointment again. Do you understand me? Your career is ruined."

"Yes, sir, I understand you," Edwards said looking blankly at the floor, and then slowly, and somewhat pathetically, added, "Sir, isn't there some way I can make things right again?"

The captain stood and thought for a few minutes. He seemed to be very carefully considering the situation. Finally, he spoke. "Edwards...look at me, man."

Edwards looked up at the captain.

"Edwards, sometimes I need a man. A man who would do anything I ask without questions and who will forget whatever he did as soon as it's done. Do you understand what I mean?"

"Yes, I understand you," Edwards said slowly, and he did understand. He understood perfectly well. The seas were a rough world with few rules that couldn't be broken, and the captain of a vessel often needed things done that he could not do himself and that no one could ever know about.

"You will be that man for me. And you will do exactly what I ask without asking any questions and without remembering any of it."

"I will, sir."

"Then I will leave you in this cell until we are underway, and then you will work the next month without pay. I will let you know when I need help with something."

"Yes, sir."

The captain turned and climbed the steep stairs upward and out of the room.

Edwards now belonged to the captain, but at least he was not ruined.

The night after he had brought Connie and Fernando back to Maria, he had trouble sleeping. He was worried that he had just made another terrible mistake. Of course, he didn't want to be the one bringing the captain bad news, but now he had broken protocol and left a stowaway in a passenger's care. He should have locked the boy in one of the cells and told the captain about it. The captain wouldn't want to feed the boy for the rest of the trip and, now that Edwards was in his debt, the captain would probably have asked Edwards to get rid of the boy. He wouldn't have specified how, he wouldn't have cared how, but Edwards would know that the boy should simply disappear into the sea. Edwards had a gruff manner, but he would never want to hurt a child. He had two daughters himself back in Devon on the southern coast of England. He was always out at sea, so he hardly saw them, but he always sent money to their mother. He knew he was not a good father; in fact, he was not really a father at all, but he wanted to do what he could. He wanted to be a better man, and he certainly didn't want to hurt a twelve-year-old who was just trying to find a better life.

All of his thoughts made it difficult to fall asleep, but eventually he did, and then in his sleep he heard a noise, well not exactly, he really felt something. He felt a presence. Someone was in the room with him. That's when he woke up and sat bolt upright. Someone was out there in the dark. He couldn't hear anything, but he felt someone. "Who's out there?" he whispered.

Edwards was surprised to hear a sensual female voice reply, "It's just me silly. Do you remember me?" A match lit and revealed the face of the beautiful woman with the red dress.

"How did you get in here?" Edwards asked; after all, ship's security was his main duty, and this was a serious breach of security. "Who let you onboard? And where have you been since we left Madeira?"

The woman walked up to him and sat down on the bed. He could feel her press up against his leg. She put her hand on his thigh. Through the blanket he felt her squeeze him softly. "There is no reason for you to get so demanding with me," she said. "I came back to see you and to ask you a few questions."

"No, you need to answer my questions. What are you doing here and how did you get onboard?" Edwards asked loudly this time.

She touched him on the side of the face, gently rubbing his cheek. "OK, I will answer your questions. I am here because I need your help, and I didn't get onboard in any ordinary way. I simply appeared right here. I am sure you find those answers somewhat less than satisfying, but they are both true. Now, I need you to start playing along, or I am going to get angry."

Edwards started to get up out of bed. He was going to put her in a cell and continue the conversation once she was locked in the hold. As he started to move, the woman grabbed him by the shoulder and forced him back down with the strength of a mountain gorilla. He was stunned. In the morning, he would find a big purple bruise on his shoulder. He was lucky she didn't break his collarbone with her grip. "Sit down," she said, her cleavage nearly bursting through the top of her dress from the exertion. "Sit down and listen."

Edwards was simply too stunned to do anything else. He just sat there, having no idea whatsoever as to what was happening.

"You found the boy. That's good, but you gave him to Maria. Why did you do that? You were supposed to throw him overboard. We had an arrangement."

"What are you talking about? I saw you for the first time at the tavern just before I smashed that kid's hand. And right now is the first time we have ever spoken. We never had any arrangement."

"I didn't let you remember, but believe me, we had an arrangement. You were going to find the boy, toss him overboard at the stern of the boat after you knocked him unconscious late at night. It was a very simple plan and you blew it."

"Listen, lady, you are crazy. I don't know what you are talking about." Edwards was confused, angry, and nervous. He didn't know how this lady had gotten in his room or on the ship. He was terrified of her inhuman strength. And he had no idea what she was talking about. And to make it all worse, he was afraid that he would be blamed for her presence onboard.

"There is only one thing I need to know from you. Who else has contacted you? Who told you to bring that boy to Maria?"

"No one told me anything. I just did that because it was the easiest solution I could see. I made that choice all on my own."

"Think about it, you simpleton." The woman was clearly angry now. "It would make no sense for you to give a stowaway to a passenger. If anyone found out that you had done that, you would be in a cell again. You are obligated to report any unaccounted-for passengers directly and promptly to the captain. Weren't you thinking all of that yourself just before you fell asleep? Isn't that what you were worrying about? Why would you give that boy to Maria if not because someone else forced you to?"

Edwards truly did not know why he had done it. And that was exactly what he had been thinking about as he fell to sleep. Why would he risk everything for that boy? It didn't make any sense to him either. "I don't know," he confessed. "It was stupid. Sometimes I do stupid things, and later I don't know why I did them."

"You were influenced," she said more to herself than Edwards, and the statement didn't make any sense to the third mate.

"Touch my breast," the lady commanded and then looked at him. He slowly reached out and touched her breast. It was firm, but soft, and on any other occasion he would have enjoyed the feeling. Then he slowly retracted his hand. "Touch it again," she said. He reached out again and touched her right breast again. This time he was shocked to find it rock hard. Her breast seemed to have solidified into stone. His hand jerked away. "Go ahead, knock on it," she said. He did. The breast was as hard as stone. It was like banging on a marble statue. "I am not human. I am more like a god to you. I have been talking to you in your dreams for a long time now. I have been guiding you through all the steps necessary to get this post, on exactly this voyage. I have invested a lot of time and energy into you, and you just blew the whole plan."

Edwards just sat. He couldn't speak. He couldn't think. He couldn't even be confused because he was just blank.

"I need to know who else influenced you. Someone stopped you from throwing the boy overboard and then convinced you to bring him to Maria, and I need to know who!" She looked into Edwards' vacant eyes. He was gone. He couldn't take it anymore. She pushed him down onto his back where he would sleep for the rest of the night. He wouldn't remember any of this in the morning. All she knew was that someone was interfering with her plan, and whoever it was, they probably had mastery of the dream realms. She knew it couldn't be Pessoa. He couldn't come here himself. But he had his minions, his heteronyms, and one of them might be here doing his bidding. Or even worse, it might be the old woman. Either way, it did not matter. Whoever it was, she would find out who, and she would destroy them along with the boy.

CHAPTER 7

Jeff and Vicente Arrive Onboard

I woke up and there was Vicente standing near the door, motioning for me to come with him. This had been the exact routine we had followed for the last fifteen consecutive nights. Pessoa stopped coming after the first night, but I remembered Vicente returning to my dreams every night thereafter. I had asked Vicente why I had to fall asleep each night before he arrived. Why couldn't I just wait up for him? He said that was exactly what we were working toward, but at this point, my mastery was too weak. I needed to allow my mind and body to fall asleep in the conventional way. Then, once sleep had removed me from the world, Vicente could connect with me while I was dreaming, and from there, he could awaken me into the dream realm, which was really a trans-dream state – a state that exists in the space between our normal dreams. I had to be dreamed awake, he would say laughing.

Over the days that we had started working together, I had been initiated into a strange understanding of reality. It was hard for me to accept at first, but Vicente was clever.

He started by explaining my life from his point of view. What he showed me was that he, or Pessoa - it was always hard for me to know if they were one person or two - had influenced all of the major turning points of my spiritual life. They had guided me to want to be a priest, and then they had led me away from the church and toward the study of lucid dreaming. When the time was right, they had awakened my interest in meditation and guided me to the Hindu teachings of Advaita Vedanta that I had followed so ardently. They had even ensured that the specific teachings of Ramana Maharshi were the ones I followed. They did all this in service of the work that Vicente and I were now doing. And this work was part of some larger goal that I only had the barest inklings of.

It took a few days, but eventually, I had to accept the truth of what he was saying because he simply knew too many facts. He knew intimate details of the external circumstances of my life, and also the subtle intricacies of my inner deliberations and consternations. I could not understand how he knew these things, but I could not deny that he did. I had to accept the fact that he and Pessoa had been influencing and guiding my life in profoundly significant ways for years. Once I accepted this, he explained that this was much more common than I would ever have imagined.

Almost everyone is influenced by a non-incarnate being at least a few times in their lives. The voices you hear in your head, the intuitive feelings, the strange spontaneous choices that we make, are sometimes evidence of trans-dimensional influences. There are nearly eight billion people on Earth, but for each of those, there are dozens of non-incarnate entities. Beings without bodies, some of whom want to influence events on Earth. It seems that life beyond the body is less interesting than embodied life, and that makes life on Earth a constant preoccupation for many wandering souls, gods, angels, and demons. The trans-dimensional realms are full of all sorts of nonmaterial entities, and many of them have an interest in human affairs on Earth, even if only to entertain them through eternity.

This has all been a little hard to swallow, but Vicente is convincing, and he has shown and done things that I cannot explain. So, I am simply going along with all this, at least for the time being. As the days went on, I became more and more obsessed with what I was learning. It started to affect my job and my relationship with Roxy. I am sure it would have affected my relationship with my friends too, but to be honest, I haven't talked to any of them in the past couple of weeks. Tonight, Vicente has promised, will be the culmination of all that we have practiced.

I followed Vicente down to the living room. Of course, we could do our work up in the bedroom with Roxy asleep right next to us, but I was more comfortable here. I knew that she would never wake up, because we were working inside my dreams, yet I still found it impossible to concentrate with her in the room. As soon as I saw Vicente standing in the light of the living room, I could see that he was different. He was solemn, almost sad today. I had become used to him being firm and demanding when we worked, but also somewhat playful. Today his dark eyes looked like they were full of uncried tears.

"What's wrong?" I asked. "You look sad."

"This is a great day for us, Jeff. We will be going on a rescue mission to save your great-grandfather, but it is a sad day too. This will not be an easy time for us, and there is no guarantee of our success." Vicente stopped there, but I knew there was more that he was not telling me. I always felt that I had about one fifth of the truth, but I had learned quickly that asking for more information would not get me any.

"He is a great man, you know," Vicente said and then paused.

"Who? Fernando?"

"Yes, Fernando Pessoa is a great man. There were only ever a handful of people who mastered the dream realms on their own, and of those, only Pessoa created a method to reliably teach others the art of dreaming. He dreamed his way to the Lady, the Lady of Dreams who is the source of all the energy in the dream realms. Pessoa loved her, and I believe, although Pessoa refuses to confirm, that he became her lover. He was the only one who was able to let go that far into the dreams. Only he was able to not just master the art of dreaming, but to become a dream of himself. Your great-grandfather was a great dreamer, one of the greatest, but he never fully entered the realm of dreaming in that way. He held onto the Earth. He stayed. Your great-grandfather was always a person who had mastered dreaming, but Pessoa became a dream that had a human attached to it. This will not make much sense to you now, but trust me, it is extraordinary."

"Pessoa always said it was only because your great-grandfather had allowed himself to get caught up in the web of the world that he remained human. Constantine married and had children. That was Pessoa's great sacrifice. He had no real friends or close family. He lived life with only acquaintances and most of them distant. He needed to keep himself unbound so that he could dream freely and, ultimately, so that he could let go of the world and become a dream.

"Think about this the next time you see him. Pessoa is not a person in the world who is dreaming. He is a dream of a human in the world. Do you understand the difference? He is not a person. He is a dream. He is not here; he is free of the world. And this is where you will need to go tonight – at least part way. You will need to liberate yourself from the world so that you can dream freely. You will not go as far as Pessoa did. You will not become the dream of a human. You will remain a person dreaming, but in the dream that you dream, you will be free to move without the heavy binds of the world.

I looked at Vicente's big, sad eyes. I knew that he was trying to explain something very important to me, and I also knew that I was understanding very little of what he was saying.

"I know," Vicente said as if reading my mind. "I speak of many things, and they all sound strange and some sound terrible. I have no one to talk to about these things, and so sometimes I just say them to you. Please remember that nothing I say should be taken literally. I use words as best I can, but they are not capable of holding the truth that they point to. If you get caught in the words, you will miss the truth. Use my words to guide your sight, but always look beyond them. Do you understand?"

"Yes, I understand, but I do have one question."

"Ask."

"If Pessoa is the greatest dream master of all time, then why am I not learning from him? Why isn't he here?"

"Pessoa cannot go on this mission, and so you and I needed to bond through all of this training because it is us who must travel together. And there is one other thing that we have not spoken about, although I know that you have already guessed at it. Pessoa and I are not two people. We are not the same person either, but we are not separate. I am a heteronym. I am a unique person, but my life is sourced from Pessoa's. Pessoa gave birth to me, and even now he lives through me, or perhaps I live through him, but I existed before I was born. I was living a life of nonexistence, and then Pessoa allowed me to take my form from him. It is really not possible for me to explain, but you are not a heteronym. You are a truly separate and independent being who dreams. Your great-grandfather believed that you would become a great dreamer, perhaps as great as Pessoa, and now Pessoa believes that as well. I am your teacher and your guide for this mission only. When we have done what we need to do, it will be Pessoa that continues your training. You will learn from the true master, and you will learn from some of his other heteronyms, but learning from his heteronyms is the same as learning from him. He is all of us, and we are all him."

"I don't know if I am glad that I asked or not. I don't understand, but I know that I am going to keep following this path until something gets clear to me. I have worked with my dreams for years, and I always felt that it was for an important reason. Perhaps this is it. Or perhaps I am simply going mad, but I must find out. Tell me what I must do, and I will do my best." I was feeling an inner resolve and a deep sense of destiny. Somehow, all of this was supposed to happen. I was supposed to be here with this strange man, in my dreams. I was born for this. I was certain of it, even though it made no sense.

"Sit with me. We are going to attempt a journey. We need to succeed. I will lead the journey. I will guide us into the dream world. You only need to follow. What you must do is let go of the world and allow yourself to be pulled along by my dreaming. You must stay absolutely calm, and you must stay absolutely detached. Any excitement at all, any emotional movement toward anything will end the dreaming. This is what makes dream travel so difficult. You can want nothing. You can feel nothing. I will initiate the dream movement, not you. At this stage of your training, it will take everything you have and more just to remain calm and detached. Do not try to do anything. I cannot say this enough. Do not try to do anything. You must use a supreme degree of single-mindedness, and that focus will generate an intense and extraordinary inner clarity." Vicente stopped there and closed his eyes. We were both sitting cross legged on the sofa which is where we often worked. "If we are successful," he added opening his eyes briefly, "you will have attained the third degree of dream mastery."

We sat in silence for nearly an hour before Vicente spoke again.

"Close your eyes," Vicente said. "You must just sit and aspire to do absolutely nothing. You must have no anticipation for anything to happen at all. You must know that nothing is going to happen and, at the same time, have no anticipation for nothing to happen. You must do absolutely nothing, but, and this is the hardest part, things will

JEFF CARREIRA

happen. You must expect nothing to happen even though you will continue to see that something is happening. You must act as if nothing is happening even while many things are happening. To learn how to do this, we start with the breath. Allow your breath to become slow and steady. Allow it to happen while relating to it as if it were not happening." Vicente stopped, and I moved my attention onto my breath. I felt my chest moving up and down. Feeling the air moving in and out of my nostrils and my mouth. We sat in silence for a long time, perhaps another hour, before Vicente spoke again.

"As you breathe, allow your body to relax completely. Don't even use any effort to hold yourself upright. If you fall over, you fall over. That does not matter. All that matters is that you relax and let go. If you are destined to fall over, you will; if you are destined to remain upright, you will. There is nothing you can do to prevent your destiny." After a few minutes more, he said, "Now allow yourself to realize that you are not breathing anymore. Breathing continues to happen, but it is not you that is breathing. Your body is breathing all by itself. Allow the activity of breathing to continue without you. Just be aware of a breathing body, knowing that it is not you that is breathing." We sat for longer in silence. I began to realize that it was indeed my body that was breathing. I wasn't doing anything. I was just aware of a body breathing. I was not breathing. I was not even the body that was breathing. I was just the awareness that was aware of the breathing and the body. My hands rested heavily in my lap. Thoughts were moving through my mind, but I was not thinking. The mind was thinking. Thoughts and feelings were proceeding along

70

habitual paths. They were rolling like rain drops along a glass surface. I was not guiding them. They were simply happening, gliding along according to a mysterious inner gravity that pulled them. I had no more control over those thoughts and feelings than I did the weather.

"Nothing that you ever thought of as your life had anything to do with you," Vicente continued. "It was all just happening. Your birth, your thoughts, your pain, your joy, were all simply the inevitable consequence of what had come before. Each occurrence pushing the next one along in an unending chain of unavoidable consequences. None of it was ever you doing anything. It was all just happening. You are learning the art of disillusion. You are undoing the universe so that it can be remade. You are learning to disconnect from reality with all of your senses. You are letting go. You are leaving a world that never existed, full of events that never happened. You are letting go of the person that was never you and was never there. There is no way to know that you do not exist. How can someone who is not there know that they are not there?"

Vicente stopped talking again. My mind swirled. I felt drunk. None of this is me. None of this is happening to me. I am not swirling, and I am not drunk. My mind is desperately trying to hold together a picture of reality that was never true. It is trying to find a way to place me in this picture. To convince me that I am confused, but I am not confused at all. I am totally clear. I see with absolute clarity the chaos of my mind losing control. Thoughts going crazy, feelings rushing through my body. Everything feels like impending doom and death. Everything feels so wrong. And in the midst of it all, there is perfect clarity and perfect peace. I don't want any of this to go away. And I don't care if it does. I have no aspiration for anything to be anything. I have lost all concern. There is nothing but what is. There is not even a person who is aware of what is. There is just what is. I feel blank. I feel empty. I don't feel at all. I can't even say that I feel blank, because blankness is something. I can't say that I feel nothing, because I don't feel at all. There is no feeling of nothing, there is simply no feeling at all. Nothing is still something, and this is the impossible opposite of that.

"Jeff, you have done well. You are gone. You have left the world completely behind. You have forgotten your own existence. You are truly dreaming now. Relax and listen. Hear the sound way in the distance. Now louder. It is a creaking sound. Listen to that sound. Give all of your attention to the sound." Vicente's voice spoke, but he was not here anymore. The voice was heard but not by me. There was no one to hear the sound of the voice, and there was no one to speak, and yet, there was a voice that spoke and it was heard. And then the sound of a creak. Creak, creak, creak, creak. Followed by a gentle splash, splash, splash, splash. A cool breeze blew across a face that wasn't there. These were sensations, pure sensations, without anyone to feel them. And yet they were there, and they were being felt. As the sounds and the feelings were felt, slowly someone developed. A person grew out of the sensations like a leaf grows out of a tree branch. A person appears only because the sensations need a person to feel them. The sensations give birth to a person. The sensations have a person, but that person does not have sensations. The sensations are first, the person is second.

Vicente and I were standing on the deck of a ship. The sun was high in the sky. It looked as though it should have been very hot, but it wasn't. The ocean stretched out to the horizon in all directions. "Where are we, Vicente?" I asked.

Vicente looked at me with a wide smile. He was clearly very happy. "We have made it, my friend. You did very well. You did very well." He leaned over and hugged me and kissed me hard on my cheek.

"You did very well," he repeated, "You did very, very well." As he moved his face away from mine, I saw tears streaming down his cheeks. My cheek was also covered with his tears. I do not believe I had ever seen someone this happy before in all my life. I looked around and saw that there were many sailors on the deck with us. None of them looked at us, but Vicente must have seen my concern.

"Don't worry," he said. "None of them can see us. We are less than a faint mist to them. You will find that almost no one will ever see you. Very occasionally, you will run into someone who is sensitive enough to see you. You will immediately wish they hadn't. They will scream and they will run. Or they will try to get someone else to see you. If you are in a crowd, they will quickly realize that they should not say anything more about you to anyone. If there is ever someone who sees you and is not afraid, then you can be sure that they are consciously dreaming like you. No one we meet here will see anything, except those that we are looking for." He paused for a moment looking up into the clear blue sky. "We made it. I can't believe we made it."

"Where are we again?"

"We are on the ship. We are on the ship with young Fernando Pessoa and his mother and your great-grandfather."

"You mean we just time traveled."

"Well, yes, I suppose we did, although we don't think in terms of time travel. You see, a master dreamer knows that all time always exists simultaneously. There is no linear time except as perceived by people with blinders on, but yes, you could also say that we have traveled back in time. I believe it is some time in January, or maybe February, of 1896."

"How will we get back?" I asked, beginning to be terrified by what I was seeing around me. "How will we get back?"

"Getting here is much harder than getting back. Take it easy and give yourself a few hours to get used to this. We can spend the rest of the day exploring the ship. Right now, you are only worried about getting back to the dead world you left behind, but soon you will realize that you have entered a new universe of multiplicity and dynamic life. Getting back to your old dream life is not difficult, but you now have an infinite number of dreams to live. You may soon not want to go back at all."

Vicente turned his head away and looked up at the sky and then said again, "You did very, very well." But this time I realized that I was not sure if he was referring to me or to himself.

Jeff's Early Explorations of the Dream Realms

DURING THE TIME THAT Vicente and I worked together, he asked me about my early experiences in lucid dreaming. He said that we had been working together during the time that I'd had some of those dreams, but now that I had been dreamed awake, he wanted to know what I remembered now from the lucid dreams I had in the past. He had a notebook that contained his notes from when he first heard about the dreams, and now he would check what I remembered about my lucid dreams against what I had originally reported. Presumably, I would remember differently when fully conscious, and in some ways more accurately, and he needed to find out the truth.

I described to him how my second lucid dream started out with a classic incongruity. The dream initiated with me at work. I was an associate engineer at a small electronics company outside of Boston that manufactured semiconductor diode lasers. This was actually true in my real life as well as in the dream. As the dream begins, I am walking down the hallway toward the restrooms. There is a short corridor off of the main hallway and the ladies' and mens' room doors are located on that corridor. As I turn into the corridor, I see a woman walking past me. She has just come out of the ladies' room.

"Hi," she says to me, and I recognize that it is my mother.

"Hi, Mom," I say in return, and then I walk into the bathroom. It isn't until I am sitting on a toilet that it hits me. "My mom doesn't work here." I thought, "This must be a dream." Suddenly, I had no need to use the restroom. It seems that you can dream of needing to use the restroom, but once you become aware that you are dreaming there is no need at all. The same goes for eating. You can dream of being hungry and you can dream of eating, but once you are awake in a dream there is no more need for food.

Because this was my second lucid dream, I was much calmer. Of course, it also wasn't a dream about being swarmed by zombies. As I sat for just a minute more, I looked at the door in front of me. Once again, I was amazed at how absolutely convincingly real it seemed. Nothing about it would betray that this was a dream and not reality. But I already knew this about dreams, so I wasn't nearly as flabbergasted as I had been in the first dream. I felt much more level-headed and curious this time. I decided that I would test out some of those things that I had read about, and I knew exactly what I wanted to test first.

I had been very intrigued by the idea that in a dream you can't look at yourself in a mirror. As I understood it, it wasn't that you wouldn't cast an image in a mirror like a vampire, it was simply physically impossible to position yourself in front of a mirror to even look. I was in a restroom. I knew there were three mirrors over the three sinks on the other side of this door, so I was in the perfect place to test the theory.

I walked out of the stall and toward the mirror. I was looking straight at the mirror from the side, but just as I was about to be able to see my own reflection I stopped. I couldn't move. I was too afraid to look. I took a deep breath and then started to move into view of my reflection. I couldn't. I simply could not move. A terror like the fear of death overcame me each time I moved closer to seeing my own reflection. I simply could not do it. It was as if I was held back by an invisible force. I was bumping up against a solid wall of terror. It felt thick. It was invisible.

Then something very strange happened. As I pressed up against it, I could hear it screaming inside. The voice of sheer terror. It was saying something. It was calling my name. "Jeff, I am here. Do not forget me. I am here. I need your help." The sound was so faint that I could not be sure that I had heard it at all, but in telling this to Vicente, he asked me to repeat it over and over again. He did not tell me why he was so interested to know exactly what I had heard. At the time of the dream, I just thought that I had misheard. The sound was barely audible, and it was simpler just to assume that it was nothing.

So, after failing to look into the mirror, I walked past them with my eyes averted, and I left the restroom and headed to my office. I sat down at my desk and picked up a book that I had in the top drawer. It was a science fiction novel by Gene Wolfe called *Free Live Free*. I opened the book randomly to page 235 and read the first few words on the page. It said, "Dr. Bob stared at her, rubbing his chin, then made a note in his pad." I closed the book for a moment with my finger still in the page, then opened it again. Now it said, "Never in her life had she experienced so much pain." I did it again, closed the book and then opened it to the same page. This time it said, "Why is it so important to you that things remain the same?" This last one I found interesting because it seemed to be directed toward me in that moment. It felt more like a direct response to what I was just now doing. I opened up the book again and it said, "I know what you are trying to do, and it will never work."

I decided to try something. This time when I closed the book, I also asked it a question out loud. "Are you speaking directly to me?" I asked. I opened the book and there was only one sentence printed directly on the center of the page, "Of course, who else would I be speaking with?" My mind began to spin hard. I felt dizzy. This book was talking to me. It had heard what I said, and it had answered. I did it again, "Can the real copy of this book in real life do this too?" I opened the book. It said, "I am the real book in your real life. There is only one of us. I can do this here in your dream, and I can do it there in your so-called real life." I closed the book and then felt compelled to open it again. This time on the page it said, "The more important question is, will you be able to hear me in your real life?"

At that moment, I started to think about how much Colleen would love all this. Colleen worked in our fabrication lab. She was one of my best friends here, and she was just as fascinated with dreams as I was. We had always said that if either of us became conscious in a dream, we would call the other into it.

I put the paperback on the desk and sat back. From what I had read, the way you call someone into your dream is to imagine them in the next room, or around a corner, or anywhere that is out of sight. Then you walk over to that place and you will find them there. I imagined Colleen in the office next door, then I got up and walked into it. There she was, sitting at the desk with her white lab coat on just as I had imagined.

"Hello, Colleen," I said.

"Hi."

"Do you know where you are?"

"Yeah. I'm at work, just like you."

"Actually, this is not work. This is a dream. I called you into it just like we said we would."

"No shit. Really?" She had exactly the response I would have hoped; receptive, surprised, and thrilled. Followed, naturally, by a dose of skepticism. "Prove to me that this is a dream," she challenged.

"Sure," I said confidently. "Tell me anything and I will materialize it here for you."

"OK, a Twinkie." Colleen loved those little cakes. The rule that governed materializing objects, I had read, was the same as the one that governed how people could be manifest in dreams. It had to happen out of sight. I put my hand behind my back and imagined a Twinkie in it. I put my hand in front of me and there was a new unopened Twinkie in it. I smiled triumphantly.

"OK," she said, "you did it."

"This is actually my second lucid dream, but I was too overwhelmed the first time to remember to get you."

"What should we do?" Colleen asked.

"I want to try something. Close your eyes and imagine something...a...a...farm. Then open your eyes and you should be there. I will do the same." I closed my eyes, imagined a farm, and then opened them. I was staring at an open field full of pumpkins. I turned around and there was a barn. Colleen was nowhere to be seen. Maybe because it was my dream, I was the only one that could do things in it. Or maybe we had just imagined different farms, and she was on her farm right now. Looking towards the barn, I saw that there were a number of people walking in and out of it. It was not just a barn. It was a farm stand, and I walked over to it.

As I approached the barn door, I passed a cart full of pumpkins. The pumpkins were stacked one on top of the other in a pile. Some were bright orange, others more pale or yellow. Some were perfect or nearly perfect in shape and color. Others were quite oddly shaped, having dents or brown spots where they had lain uncomfortably on the ground. You might expect that in a dream all the pumpkins would look more uniform and generic, but not so. Just like in real life, the pumpkins in dreams came in all shapes, sizes, and qualities.

I walked into the front door of the barn and saw that the inside had been converted into a country store. There were tables with rows of jars of fruit jams and preserves. There were shelves selling cookies and crackers and cakes and breads. There was a small coffee bar in the back of the barn. There were only a few people in the barn right now. An older lady with her gray hair tied up behind her head was pushing a cart filled with items she had picked out. Behind the checkout counter there was an attractive young woman. She had shoulder length hair and a pretty smile. As I got closer to her, I could see that her face was a bit pimply, but that didn't at all detract from the overall sense that she was attractive. Why? I wondered. Why give a girl in a dream a pimply face? Who was making these decisions? Was my unconscious just randomly generating people or was there some reason and purpose as to why things show up in dreams the way they do? Did this girl need to have a pimply face? Was it some kind of a symbol or message for me?

"Hello," I called out to the girl with the pimply face as I walked up to her.

"Hello," she said back. "How are you today?"

"I'm good, thank you."

"Can I help you with anything?" she asked.

"I really just want to tell you something." She looked at me curiously and with just a hint of uncertainty. "I want to tell you that this is not real. Right now, you and I are in one of my dreams."

Now she looked more concerned than curious. "Excuse me?"

"I am dreaming right now, and you are a character in my dream. You are not a real person; you are a construct of my imagination." I was getting very excited. I felt that if I could just convince her that she was not real, then I could bring her with me into reality. She would become an access point to my unconscious mind, or maybe the collective unconscious, or divine wisdom, or something like that. She just looked at me blankly.

"Do you understand what I am saying?" I asked, but she didn't move. She was frozen. Her mouth was half open as if she were about to speak. Her right eye was halfway closed. She had both hands on her hips. She was completely frozen.

I looked around the barn and saw the old lady still wheeling her cart and filling it with items to purchase. I ran over to her. "Hello," I called out.

"Hello, young man," she said.

I stopped in my tracks. I knew this woman. It was the nun from Paris who had been baking muffins in the stone tower room. "It's you!" I exclaimed.

"Has been all day," she cracked. "You're you too, I presume."

"Do you know that this is all a dream?" I asked.

"Of course, I know this is all a dream. Do you think I would ever willingly come to a farm stand to buy all this crap?" She waved her hand to point out the cart full of items she was wheeling around.

"Look," I said pointing to the now frozen pimply girl.

"Yes, I saw you trying to explain to her that she was only a dream character. I thought she lasted quite a few minutes actually. You see, that is what happens when you confront an unconscious construct with conscious awareness. It freezes. Well, at least if you do it as abruptly and unskillfully as you were doing." Then her tone changed, and she mocked me, "I am dreaming right now, and you are a character in my dream." She paused and looked at me. "What did you think was going to happen?"

"Are you in all my dreams?" I asked, partly because I didn't like being made fun of.

"I'm in a lot of them. I guess you could say that I am a little like a guardian angel, well a dream aspect of a guardian angel. I watch out for you. I try to scare off any malevolent influences that are trying to shape your life. Of course, things are going to get more complicated now that you are waking up in here. Makes my job more difficult, and it will make you a bigger target for energies that want to find a way into the world. There have been two men exerting influence over you for a long time. One of them is actually coming to you as two aspects of themselves – he is a truly great dreamer who is trying to protect your great-grandfather. The other one is also a great dreamer, but he is obsessed with the forces of darkness. He is not trying to harm you, he needs your help desperately, but dealing with him is more dangerous because of his obsession."

"I don't know what you are talking about," I interrupted.

"I know you don't, but you will soon enough. I just want to tell you something, and you will remember this; be careful with all of them, especially the one who is infatuated by darkness. They have a reputation here in the dreams. I haven't dealt with them before, but I am asking you to be careful with both of them. I could be wrong about them, but it will be best for you if you keep your eyes open." Then she added, "And, don't tell them that I told you that." She finished and then changed the subject. "And you shouldn't wake people up in a dream and then leave them."

"What?" I asked.

"Like your friend Colleen. You just left her behind."

"Left her where?" I asked confused.

"Left her in the dream. You brought her into the dream realm and then you left her. That's not good, it will come back to haunt you. She will be looking for you and sooner or later she will find you. When you leave someone behind, you create an aspect. The Colleen that you brought into the dream cannot return to her waking life without you. She is not in a natural dream that ends. She is in a deliberately manifested dream. She is now a double of her waking self, separately alive in the dream realms. At first, she will want to return to wholeness. She will seek passionately for a return to herself, but over time she will become identified with her new aspect, and she will cherish her independence and fight fiercely to protect it. You, as the manifester of the aspect, become a threat because you can return her to wholeness. You can send her back to her original self and now she does not want to go. She will eventually feel that, for her own protection, she needs to hunt you down and kill you. Do you see what you have done?"

"She was supposed to follow me," I said weakly in my defense.

"It doesn't work that way. If you wanted to bring her here, you would have needed to hold on to her body or at least her clothes. You need to make a direct connection. Anyway, you didn't, and now she's just sitting in that office wondering where you went, but eventually she will start looking."

"How do you know all this?" I asked.

"I made the same mistake once. And I am still paying for it," she said solemnly.

"Should I go back for her?" I asked with an invigorated sense of urgency.

"Not now, we have more important things to attend to, but you will need to come back for her eventually. She'll be OK for now. But we have no time, I just wish you had not called her. We have other things, much more pressing, that we need to talk about, but let's not do it here." She looked around the barn, which was starting to get crowded with customers. The pimply girl was still frozen behind the counter.

"Will she be OK?" I asked, gesturing toward the pimply girl.

"Yes, she is naturally dreaming, as soon as you're gone, she'll pick up right where she left off before she saw you," she said. "Let's go back to the stone tower where we met in our last lucid dream. I prefer that," the older woman said, taking his hand.

When I reported this dream to Vicente, he was very interested in the old lady. He wanted to know every detail that I could remember. He said that Pessoa and he had been tracking this lady down for a long time. They believed that she was one of the most powerful of the Elementals. They felt that she might be the one leading the others against human freedom. He was also very interested in the man behind the wall of fear. Neither he nor Pessoa had encountered such a thing before. Again, he asked me repeatedly to state and restate everything that I could remember. I never told him that she had warned me about the man of darkness as well as Vicente and Fernando.

CHAPTER 9

Jeff Sees Constantine's Prayers

MY GREAT-GRANDFATHER, CONSTANTINE AN-
DRADE, died when I was twelve years old. The last few
years of his life he spent in a nursing home. My family and
I would visit him once a week or so, at least once a month.
By that time, he was losing his mind. He would see things.
He would talk to me and ask me if I could see the dancing
ladies. He would be looking up at the ceiling of the room.

"Do you see them?" he would ask expectantly. "Do you
see them twirling in their dresses? Do you see the roses in
their hair? They are so beautiful. That is the way we used to
dance in the old country. Do you see them?"

I didn't see them. I would look up and sometimes I
would pretend to see them, but I think he knew that I
didn't. Of course, now, I believe he was seeing them. I don't
think he was losing his mind at all. I think he was leaving
the material world and entering into the dream world. He
wasn't seeing things that weren't there. The rest of us were

not seeing things that were. Now that I have been initiated into the art of dreaming, I realize that Constantine, or
Voovoo as all the great-grandchildren called him, was more
than he appeared to be.

After I started working with Vicente, he asked about
Voovoo a lot, he wanted to know what I remembered.
There was one story that I told him, and after that, he
wanted me to repeat it over and over again. I didn't remember much of it, but each time he asked I seemed to
remember a little more.

I was so small that I was wearing pajamas with feet in
them. They zipped up the front all the way to my neck
with only my head sticking out. They were red and they
had little football players running all over them. They were
my favorite pajamas. I remember coming down the stairs
one morning. I think it was a time when my parents left us
with our grandparents for the weekend. Voovoo lived with
my grandparents in a small room off of the kitchen.

I heard mumbling in Portuguese through the bedroom
door. I opened the door halfway so that I could see inside.
Voovoo was kneeling with his elbows resting on the bed
and his hands clasped around his rosary beads. His head
pointed down in prayer. I would do this often. Just come
and watch him pray. I said my prayers at night before bed,
but his prayers were very long. Sometimes he prayed for
an hour. I didn't understand Portuguese, so I didn't know
what he was saying.

I am sure he knew I was watching, but he never stopped
me. I imagine that he thought it was good for me to see
him pray. One day while I was watching, he turned toward
me and waved for me to come closer. I walked slowly to-

ward him in my red pajamas. When I stood next to him, he put his arm around me. Then he pointed to two pictures that hung on the wall over the side of his bed.

"Those are the two greatest men of all time," he said to me in this thick Portuguese accent. "Jesus Christ and João Kennedy."

I looked up at the photos. I knew that one, Jesus, was the son of God, and the other, Kennedy, had been the president of the United States. Even at such a young age, I instinctively felt that there was a big difference between the two.

It was the briefest of memories. There was nothing more to it, but Vicente kept asking me about it. Three days in a row he asked until finally I did begin to remember more.

"Yes, I think there is more," I said on the third day of his asking. "I can't really remember it, but I can sense more, just beyond what I know."

"Yes, that's it. Don't try to remember. Remembering means trying to see something that is already in your memory, something that you knew once, but have now lost contact with. When you remember consciously, you are just reconnecting with something that you already knew. This is different. Now you are trying to see something that was there at the time, but that you never saw then. When you remember, you tend to look inside, but in the kind of remembering that we are trying to do now, you need to look forward, not backward. You need to put yourself back in the scene of the memory and look around again now. This is not really remembering, so Pessoa calls it illuminating. You are illuminating something that was there at the time you were with your great-grandfather, but that you didn't see then. It was never stored in memory. So, you can't remember it and you never will. Remembering means calling something back to mind, but you cannot remember this because it was never in your mind to begin with."

Vicente looked at me and could see that, although I understood what he was saying, I was not getting the implications in terms of what he wanted me to do now. I was trying to follow him, but I was getting lost and he knew it.

"OK, I'm sorry I am saying too much at once. The reason why I am so excited is because this is the whole point. This distinction, the one between remembering and illuminating, is the key to mastering the fourth stage of the art of dreaming. It is the difference between calling something to mind versus traveling somewhere through the use of your mind. I know that you are very, very close to being able to do this. I just need you to pay a great deal of attention right now and work with me. Do you need some water?" he asked.

"No, I am fine. Keep going," I said.

"When we experience something, our mind creates a memory," he said, now speaking slowly and deliberately. "A memory is like a copy, or a recording. That copy gets filed in your brain and eventually forgotten about, but you do have it somewhere. It's inside you, and so when you want to remember it, you look inside until you find it. But memories record very little of what actually is. Let me use an example. Imagine you go to a symphony. It's beautiful. The most beautiful music you have ever heard. The orchestra is playing in perfect unison. The audience is sitting in rapt attention. You pull out your phone and record. A month later, or maybe a year, you listen to what is on the phone. The recording does not even come close to capturing the experience. Not only is the phone not able to capture the full quality of the sound, but there was so much more to the experience than just the sound. Listening to the recording might remind you of how much you loved that night, but it cannot recreate the event."

"That makes sense," I offered.

"Think about how little of that actual night was recorded on your phone. Even if you recorded video, you could only see what the camera was pointing to, and you can only hear what the microphone picked up. On that evening, you were aware of the people around you. You were aware of the smell in the air; you were aware of the feeling of the chair. Someone weeping in awe of the music. You were with friends sharing approving glances. Or maybe holding your girlfriend's hand. There was so much more going on that night than your phone recorded."

I nodded. It was simple and it made sense.

"That is how each and every moment is. You are always seeing more than your memory can record and, and this is the most important part, there is always so much that you are seeing in the moment that you are not even aware that you are seeing. So, on one level, your memory cannot even record all of what you know you are aware of, and on a deeper level, you are aware of much more than you are even aware of knowing. In each and every moment, we are aware of layers and layers of reality that we never consciously recognize. You are seeing things right now that you have no idea about."

"OK," I said. "I'm starting to see what you mean. There is a YouTube video." I stopped. "Do you know what a YouTube video is?"

"Yes, I try to keep up with things even if I don't use them."

"Well there is a YouTube video and it is a video of a group of dancers. You watch a short dance routine. At the end of the video, it tells you to watch again and notice the dancing bear. When you watch the video again you see that, behind the row of dancers, in the front there is also someone dressed in a bear suit that slowly dances along the back wall moving from the right side of the screen to the left. You would swear that bear was not in the video the first time you watched, but it must have been. Once you are told to look for it, then it is obvious, but before you started looking for it, you didn't see it at all."

"Yes, yes, very good. That's it exactly, except imagine a thousand dancing bears all around you all the time. That's how much of reality you are missing."

"I see," I muttered half to myself, thinking deeply about the implications of what he was saying.

"Now I don't want you to try to remember more of what happened that day. That would be like listening harder to the recording on your phone to relive the experience of the night. Instead, I want you to return to that moment and actually relive it. Your memories exist in this moment, but I need you to actually go back to that moment and tell me what you see."

I sat quietly and closed my eyes.

"I know you can do this," Vicente said.

With my eyes closed, I could smell my great-grandfather's aftershave lotion. I felt my feet wrapped in the booties of my pajamas. I wiggled my toes and felt the soft material around them. Now I felt Voovoo's arm around my waist.

I opened my eyes.

I was looking up at the photos. One of John, João , Kennedy sitting in the oval office with an American flag behind him. The other of Jesus, just his face with a soft glowing halo hovering over his head. Jesus' soft eyes looked sad; Kennedy's looked receptive but alert. I looked over and saw the rough stubble of Voovoo's beard.

"Oh, you're awake, I see," said Voovoo, turning toward me and looking into my eyes.

"Yes, I am," I said as if I had been asked a question. It was strange to hear my four-year-old voice coming out of my mouth. I remembered it perfectly. It was definitely my voice.

"Good, now turn around. Do you see someone on the bed behind you?

There were two beds in Voovoo's bedroom. One against one wall, one against the other. The other bed had been my Uncle Jimmy's before he got married and moved out. As I turned slowly, I did see someone. It was Fernando Pessoa. He had a similar broad-brimmed hat on his head, still tilted to the right, and a dark gray, almost black, coat. He wore the same round, wire framed eyeglasses. He looked a bit younger than the Fernando that had come to my bedroom, but only a little, and it was definitely him.

"Hello, Fernando," I said.

"Hello, Jeff. It is good to see you here. This must mean that our plan is moving forward."

"Don't you already know that?" I asked. "I saw you only a few nights ago."

"Time does not work the same way with us, but yes, to answer your question, I did know, but your arrival confirms the fact."

"Vicente seemed to think it was important that I come here, I presume to meet you," I said.

"It is. It is very important indeed, but it was not really to meet me that you are here. We are both here to meet with your great-grandfather. He claims to have many things to explain to us. And he is the one that called us both here," answered Pessoa. I noticed that Voovoo just sat and watched.

" Right now, you are on the ship with Vicente," Pessoa went on. I started to protest, but he waved me off. "I know you don't know this yet, but it doesn't change the fact. Right now, you are on the ship with Vicente, and it is the same ship that Connie and I took to South Africa together many years ago. So, we," he motioned to include the three of us in the room, "are all together on that ship, and my mother and Vicente are there too. Now, at the very same time, you are about to visit that stone tower room with the old lady that you told Vicente about. She seems to be very interested in you and it makes me nervous. I don't know who she is. I see her only occasionally in the realms and always cloaked behind a veil of secrecy. Whoever she is, she has attained great mastery, which is why I believe she is an Elemental. I said that I have seen her only rarely, but that was only true until very recently, suddenly she is showing up everywhere." He paused.

"She is most definitely an Elemental, but I have never heard of her in any of the dream realm histories. I know that she warned you about me and Vicente." He looked pleased with himself for somehow knowing something that I had tried to keep from him. "It seems she doesn't trust me, and to be honest with you, I don't blame her. Why should she? She is an Elemental, and my entire life is devoted to liberating human beings from people like her." As he said this, he spoke with dramatic authority, and he even turned his head upward toward heaven as if he were consecrating a sacred vow. He continued, "The Elementals are nothing more than disembodied souls from so long ago that we have all forgotten their Earthly lives. They were all human once, a long, long time ago. Why not just admit it and step down off of their imagined pedestals? Why pretend to be something more than what you are? Why exert control over the living and the realms?" He sounded truly disgusted.

"Anyway, I finally need to tell you what I know and explain what all this is about." He emphasized the phrase 'what I know', and as he said it, looked over at Constantine as if suggesting that my great-grandfather might know considerably more than he did. "You have already heard about the many, many, entities that coexist with humans without our poor ignorant race having any idea about them. They are all around us all the time, more often than not ignoring us entirely, but not always. Many of them get involved with our lives. They guide and direct us. Sometimes they are working for our benefit, other times they are using us to serve their own ends. Much more than you might imagine we are being directed through life like puppets on a string.

"My mother, Connie, and I made a discovery on that voyage to South Africa. We discovered how to consciously let go of the body and enter the dream realm. Connie had been doing it already. His fear of his uncle had forced him to find a way to escape. He escaped into dreams, not normal dreams, but dreams that occurred in other dimensions of reality and could even create new realities. My mother, through a shrewd line of questioning, worked out how he did it. Then she attempted to duplicate what he did. She didn't know it, but Connie and I made our own attempts. And we were successful once." Pessoa addressed Voovoo then, "Isn't that right, Connie?"

"It is, Fernando," my great-grandfather said, still maintaining mostly silence.

"Later we would continue our practice during the three years that Connie continued to live with us in South Africa. During those years, worlds of possibility opened up to us. We discovered the shocking truth of how many entities and beings were actually living with us, and often through us, all the time. I did not want to be controlled or even influenced by any other being. I wanted to be free. I practiced and practiced until I liberated myself from confinement in the so-called real world.

"It is commonly written about in religious traditions that in the real world we live as a body, and in the heavenly realm of spirit we live as a soul. What is not known is how many other dimensions there are, each containing another equally real aspect of ourselves. I wanted to live in all of them. I wanted to move freely from one dimension to another, from one 'self' to another. I wanted to map out a geography of consciousness and of our many selves. I realized that this was a spiritual science that must be explored. It is the ultimate science of the human interior. We need to understand the full scope of who we are. We need to gain access to all of those many aspects of ourselves. We are not one, we are many, but as long as we remain ignorant of any part of ourselves, that part can be exploited and manipulated by those who travel freely between dimensions."

"I liberated myself. I now travel freely through dimensions. I create worlds and I leave them behind fully inhabited. I had suspected from the start that someday I would discover what we have called God, and I knew that I would discover that this too is just another way that we experience ourselves in yet another dimension of being. And that is what I found. I, I myself, am the only reality that exists. Just like you are the only reality that exists. You see each person is a sole reality and everything exists within them. I am not separate from you. I am a part of you. And you are not separate from me. You are a part of me. When I see you, I see a part of myself. When you see me, you see a part of yourself. Each of us is our own unique universe, everyone else exists as part of our being, and yet we are each absolutely alone."

"Once I liberated myself, I began a quest to liberate all souls. I wanted to see every human being fully aware of their true being and free to roam freely from dimension to dimension. When all human beings knew themselves and were free from the bondage of the material world, they would no longer be vulnerable to manipulation and control. I have liberated many souls, but in my time, it was difficult to spread the work far. But, in your time, with all of your technology, I believe that we have the chance to spread the work beyond anything I could imagine. Connie believes that we need you for that, and I believe he is right. I doubted it at first, but now that I see how hard someone is trying to stop us, I can only imagine that it must be true."

"It is true!" I was shocked to hear the voice of my great-grandfather speak so ferociously. I had only ever remembered him as a soft-spoken man, but suddenly he had the energy of a lion.

"Tell us, Connie. Tell us your secret," Fernando said, yielding to the older man. Yes, Constantine was so much older than Pessoa, at least in body, because Pessoa had not aged since the moment of his death in the physical dimension of the Earth. "Tell us your secret," he said again.

CHAPTER 10

Constantine Saves Tio Marco

"I NEVER TOLD FERNANDO or his mother, Maria, how I learned the art of dreaming," my great-grandfather said to the four-year-old me. "I let them believe that I had discovered it out of the extreme duress of living with Tio Marco. And I have not told Fernando to this day, although now I suspect that you have guessed that I had a teacher. A dream master who taught me the art." He glanced over at Fernando.

"Yes," Fernando replied, "I had begun to suspect that."

"I do not know who the teacher was, but I believe that he was somehow psychically linked to the old woman, and she had something to do with saving my life, and I have come to believe that she is also influencing Jeff's development into mastery as well," Constantine said looking at me again. "I had a dream master, and I believe that my master learned from the old woman. She taught me, and then I taught Fernando and his mother. So yes, I have come to believe that the old lady taught all of us the art of dreaming, but I have no proof beyond the power of my own intuition."

"I have no idea how that is possible," Pessoa said, "but I began to suspect that something like that was why you were insisting that this meeting take place and why Jeff had to be included." Pessoa nodded in the direction of the four-year-old me in front of him. "But tell me, Connie, who is the old woman? Why do you think she is the source of our dream mastery?"

"That, Pessoa, I do not know. I suspect it because the one who taught me would occasionally mention his master. He would refer to her as his spiritual mother, and when that woman started to appear so mysteriously, I had a strong sense that I had at last met my spiritual grandmother."

Then I broke into the conversation. "How am I involved? What is my connection with the old woman?" It was again very strange to hear my four-year-old voice speaking through my mouth. It felt odd and alien to hear my own words and emotions expressed through the mouth of a child.

"Again, you are asking me questions that I cannot answer, but she has contacted you in your dreams more than once, and I suspect that you have met with her more times than that. It cannot be a coincidence that you are my great-grandson, and you so obviously have the gift of dreaming, and she is in contact with you. Something must be bringing all of us together."

I noticed that Fernando was now looking at me. It was the first time that I had seen real surprise on his face. He was shocked to learn that there might be so much more going on than he had realized.

"How is that possible?" Fernando interrupted Connie, almost angrily. "Is the old woman an Elemental as I suspect?"

"No, Fernando, you are wrong. You must now listen to me. This story will unfold, but know this, there are more human dream masters than just you. I realize this is a shock to you and not welcome news, but it is true. I knew this day would come. I knew that a day would come when I would need to tell you this story, and I must tell you now because we are all needed for a battle where we will fight, not against, but with the Elementals." Connie finished his last statement and paused for Fernando's response.

Fernando was silent for a long time, and then he began to speak slowly. "I think before I say more, I need to hear the story. I need to hear everything you know."

Connie began his story. "The first time I met my master was on the day the fire started. I was out in the fields picking vegetables when I saw smoke rising up from Tio Marco's house. I ran as fast as I could to the little house, a one room shack really, where Marco lived. One wall of the house was ablaze. As I got closer to the house, I stopped and just looked. The morning sun was bright, and the blue sky was clear. I could hear the roaring of the fire, and I could see the flames licking the wooden wall of the house. They were dancing upward toward the heavens. The paint was peeling off, and the wood underneath was turning black. I looked and I thought that it was beautiful. The flames, the smoke, the fact that my evil uncle was inside, soon to be dead. I just stopped and watched. I felt that my liberation was coming. I would soon be free of Tio Marco. And that is when my master arrived." My great-grandfather looked straight at me now, and he saw the glassy look in my four-year-old eyes. "I see that my dream is calling you. Go ahead, boy, go in and see it from the inside."

...

Suddenly I was not in the room speaking with my great-grandfather anymore. I had slipped into the scene that my great-grandfather described. And although I remembered none of it, it was all oddly familiar. I was standing in an open field looking at a house burning. I saw the young Constantine looking at the house, standing transfixed with an eerie smile on his face. He was happy, but this was wrong. This was not the way. I knew that I was not supposed to reveal myself to him yet, that this was not supposed to happen, but I had no choice; I had to risk revealing myself too soon or everything would be lost.

"Connie, no!" I shouted at the boy. "This is not the way. This is not how you free yourself from Tio Marco. He must not die this way; you must not live with the guilt of this death. You must save him!"

The boy looked at me. His eyes opened wide as he saw me. "Who are you?" he asked. As the boy looked up at me, I realized that I was much taller than he was. I was no longer in my four-year-old body. I raised my hand near my face so that I could see it. It was different. The skin was dark-colored and rough. It was a beautiful and strong hand, but it was not mine. I glanced around instinctively to find a mirror, of course there was none outside of the house... the house! It was still burning.

"Who are you?" the young Connie repeated.

"That does not matter now," I said, forgetting all about the dark-skinned hand that now seemed to reside at the end of my arm. "You must go in and wake your uncle, you must save him!" I shouted. "Go!"

The boy ran into the house. Once inside, he saw his uncle passed out on the couch, not too near to the burning wall. He ran up to his uncle and shook him. His eyes opened slightly. He was so drunk he had no idea what was happening. "Tio!" the boy shouted. "You must get up, there is a fire. You must get up!" Tio Marco's eyes opened wide. The fear from seeing the house ablaze burst through his nervous system and seemed to knock all of the alcohol out of him. He stood up and ran out of the house, leaving the young boy behind.

When Marco was a safe distance from the house, he stopped and turned to look at Connie. "What have you done! What have you done, boy!" Connie had never seen Marco so angry. "You burned down my house with me inside. It is lucky I woke up or you would have killed me. I should never have taken you in. I give you everything, and you try to kill me."

The beating that Connie received was the most brutal ever. The scene was surreal. The little house was burning. The well was only fifty feet away, but Marco was so busy beating the boy that he didn't even bother to put out the flames. The blows that young Connie received were knocking him from side to side and then he fell, and Marco started kicking him. The whole time Marco screamed, "You were going to burn me alive. What is wrong with you, boy? You are the son of the devil. Why did I ever let you in my house?" Marco surely would have continued until the boy's body was lifeless, but it was at this moment that he noticed the well and he ran for the bucket. He went back and forth with buckets filled with water until the fire was out. He looked around, but the boy was gone. And the boy would not return for over a month, and when he finally did, something would be different. He would no longer try to win his uncle's approval. He just tried to stay away from Marco as much as possible. When his beatings came, as they inevitably did, he just accepted them. He was no longer invested in being happy on the farm. Something had changed; he was living somewhere else now. And he would live in that semi-detached way until the one day when he disappeared forever.

...

The four-year-old Jeff was standing in his red pajamas staring at his great-grandfather again, who was sitting on his bed underneath the photos of João Kennedy and Jesus Christ. He had never heard such an adult story about real hardship and pain. He felt fear in his body. He could not move. The adult self that had been with him earlier was now gone, only the child remained.

Slowly, the adult mind returned. I, the adult self, was feeling his fear, but I was also seeing it from the outside. It was a very strange feeling to be both inside a person seeing through them, and outside of them watching them. Constantine looked intently at the boy... at me. "You are back.

That is good. I want to see you there as I tell you the rest of the story."

Constantine continued his story. "Marco was running back and forth with buckets full of water, and I was lying down on the ground. Each time he got close to the house, Marco would toss the water onto the burning wall. It would take many buckets before the fire was out. I was in so much pain. My ribs were broken, and my arm was broken in three places. I was bruised from head to toe and every little movement hurt. I just laid on the ground and moaned. I wished that I had let the fire burn. Why did that man make me go in for Tio Marco? And where was that man? Why had he not stopped Marco from beating me? It was all his fault really. He should have helped."

As the older Constantine described his pain and anguish, the eyes of the four-year-old in red pajamas went dull again, and once again he was gone, escaping the fear by slipping into his adult perception now transfixed in another time and place.

...

I could smell the smoke. I could hear the flames burning wildly. Marco was running with another bucket of water. He threw it against the side of the house. The water sizzled and the flame died down for a moment, but a moment later it was back unabated. I ran over to the boy. He was in so much pain.

"Get up, Connie!" I said. "Get up, we must get out of here before your uncle has put out the fire. Run this way."

Connie slowly got up and started running behind me. He was limping badly, but fear kept him running fast. "Yes, that's good. I know where we can go, it is far, but you can make it."

We ran out of the edge of the farm and down toward the water. We scrambled up on to the rocks of the shore and kept moving along the coast. Anytime I reached in front of me I saw those dark rough hands. I saw that I was not in a body that I recognized, but there was not time to stop and consider. We must keep going. The rocks became steeper and we had to move slowly and carefully, but it did not matter because it was unlikely that Marco would suspect that we had come this way, and he could not follow us even if he guessed. We did not speak, but we had to stop several times when the boy needed to catch his breath. Breathing with his ribs broken was very difficult, and he was not able to get all of the oxygen that he needed.

It took almost three hours, but eventually we came to the place. It was a cave formed by two rocks. Inside, it was dry and well protected from the wind. Connie followed the man into the small entrance, and once he was inside, he saw a small fire burning. He had no idea how the man had started a fire so quickly. The fire seemed to burn completely without smoke. It was the beginning of winter, and even though it was not cold in Madeira, the warmth from the fire felt good. Near to the fire was a mattress. It was soft.

"Lay down there and sleep," the man said to the boy as he entered the entrance to the cave. "You are tired, and you are in pain. Lay down and go to sleep."

The boy lay down and fell asleep. He woke later and saw the man chanting over him. He was sweating and he felt sleepy.

"Go back to sleep," the man said. "You will feel better when you wake up."

...

Once again, I was back in my four-year-old body with feet in my pajamas, looking up at my great-grandfather.

"Please try to be stable. You keep going back and forth. You need to stay here with me." Constantine handed me a crucifix from his night table. "Hold this. The feeling of it in your hand will help keep you grounded." Of course, as a four-year-old, I had no idea what he was saying, but as the adult self who was also listening, I knew what he wanted. He wanted me to remain present. He needed to know that I was understanding him, and he needed to be able to talk with me and ask me questions as the story unfolded.

"Yes, I will stay here," I said through my four-year-old mouth.

Connie continued his story. "I woke up after a few days, and we stayed in that cave for almost another month. During that time, the man who was with me taught me the art of dreaming and told me that I needed to learn it for a very important reason."

"What reason?" Pessoa asked. "What were you supposed to do?"

"I am not sure, just let me tell the story as I know it. Follow me as best you can," he instructed. "The man taught me to dream in that cave, and he seemed to know exactly why he was doing it and why it was so important. For some reason, there is a link between that man and Jeff here. That is why Jeff keeps slipping into his body. Jeff, I need you to illuminate what happened during that time that I was asleep in the cave. I need you to go back consciously now and see what happened so we can all discover what this is all about," Connie said and then added, "You have to understand that I was never told much. The man who was with me, the one that I suspect is somehow connected to you, never gave me the whole story. We need that story now. The reason we needed you here was because I believe that your connection to that man will allow you to merge with him at that time and illuminate for us all that he knew. And the fact that you can barely stay in the room while I tell the story confirms that I am correct."

It seemed that this was as much of the story as Fernando Pessoa was willing to take in silence. "Why have you never told me any of this before?" he demanded, suddenly interjecting himself into the flow of the conversation. He had been sitting listening to the whole story without speaking, but finally he was demanding answers. "All these years, first in life, and then in the dream realms, and never once did you tell me any of this. Why not? Why did you keep this from me?"

Constantine looked over at his friend with a gentleness in his eyes. "I could not tell you until now. Or I should say, I told you all I could. I told you that the boy was special. I told you that there was a very important reason for our learning to dream. I told you that we needed the boy to help us. I even told you that our destiny was intimately intertwined with his. I could not tell you who the man was, because I simply don't know. I could not tell you that there was another   dream master because that would have aroused your pride, and when your pride is pricked, you are unpredictable. It was always possible that you would inadvertently reveal us to forces that want to stop us."

"Connie, my oldest and best friend, I suddenly see that you have always known much more than I thought. You were always so quiet. I thought it was simply your manner. I thought that being uneducated and growing up on that island had left you with a bit slow of mind, but now I feel that I have been deceived. You are not a simple man at all, you are deep and complex. You have secrets that you have never told. I do have one question, why now? After all these years, why are you telling me now?"

"I am not sure why the time is now." Constantine explained, "I have not been told why. I can only imagine that there is some dire need because I have always been told that absolute secrecy was paramount, and so there must be very grave circumstances that necessitate us to come out in the open. But I feel in my heart that the time is now. I feel it with a sense of destiny that cannot be denied."

"Told by who? You speak as if you have been in contact with someone all this time. Who has been giving you all this information?" Pessoa demanded.

Constantine's tone became calm. "I don't want you to be angry, Pessoa. I would have told you if I could. Yes, I have had contact periodically with a woman who told me just what I needed to know at the time. And she always emphasized that I should tell no one, and that everything she said, which honestly was never much, must be kept in the strictest confidence. She has not come for a long time, but I believe that this feeling of knowing that the time is now is her influence on my soul."

"Who, who is this woman?" Pessoa said banging his fist on the bed where he sat.

"Pessoa, I will tell you all, but I must tell the whole story. It will not be helpful for me to answer to your interrogation. Please be patient. Soon you will know everything that I know." Constantine paused and waited for a response.

Pessoa relaxed for a minute, seemingly composing himself, and then said, "In spite of my feelings of betrayal, I trust you. If you felt that you needed to keep this secret, then I trust it was for good reason. But continue, we need to hear all that you know."

CHAPTER 11

Constantine Tells His Secret

"FERNANDO, EVERYTHING THAT I learned about the art of dreaming in that cave I have shared with you already. I swear there is nothing that I held back about that. During those three weeks on the ship with you and your mother, I shared everything with you. I tried to recreate the lessons I learned step by step as faithfully as I could. You mastered them much faster than I had. Perhaps that was because of some influence of your aunt. I do not know. But you and your mother mastered what I had to teach very quickly. And later you took the art of dreaming to heights that none of us could have imagined." He nodded toward the four-year-old in pajamas for no apparent reason except to acknowledge his presence. "That is part of what is so dangerous. You are one of the most accomplished human dreamers that ever entered the dream realms, and you are not an Elemental. You and a few other master human dreamers are creating an imbalance in the structure of power, or at least you are seen that way by many Elemental forces. Some of those forces see you as a threat that must be stopped."

At hearing mention of other human dreamers as accomplished as he, Pessoa's expression soured. "Who else has mastered the dream realms as I have?" he questioned. "I have heard of no such human dreamers in all my years of extensive dream travel."

"Two I think you will be meeting soon. One of those you have not heard of because he inadvertently imprisoned himself in nightmares of terror from which he cannot escape. The other is a woman who has chosen to hide herself until the appointed time. She is my master's masters, and she is the old lady in contact with Jeff." Constantine stopped for a moment before continuing. "The old lady is not an Elemental as you assumed. She is a human dreamer, like you. And it appears that the time has come for you and her to meet."

Fernando was irritated with all of this talk of other dreamers as accomplished as he. He did not like sharing this distinction with strangers. He looked unapprovingly first at Constantine and then at the small boy in pajamas.

Constantine continued, "Before I speak of her, I must tell you a secret about myself. A secret that I fear you will not like in the least."

"So far, I have enjoyed very little of what you have to say today. I don't know why the next thing would be any different," Pessoa said.

"Fernando," Constantine continued as if he had not heard Pessoa's remark, "I suspect that I am not human."

Fernando stopped dead. He looked straight at Constantine and said just one word, "Elemental?"

"I do not know if I am an Elemental. I suspect that I am not human," Constantine said slowly.

The young boy watched as the two men spoke. His four-year-old mind had no idea what was being spoken of, but the much older mind of his adult self that was also present inside him was beginning to understand a great deal.

Constantine continued to speak as Pessoa sat frozen with a brimming silent rage beginning to overtake his countenance. "My initial memory of the events after the fire was that I followed the dark-skinned man to the cave on the coast. While I slept for a number of days, he healed me. Once I was healed, he trained me in the art of dreaming. Later I went back to Tio Marco, who was genuinely overjoyed to see that I had survived. He told everyone that it was a gift from God in answer to his prayers. He had promised God that he would not drink another drop of alcohol if I returned and he would treat me like gold. For a few months, things were very different between Tio Marco and I; he did not drink, and he did not hit me, but eventually things went back to the way they had been. He was drinking again and beating me regularly." At this point he stopped briefly. "That," he said with emphasis, "is what I remembered and all that I remembered during the time that I knew you in South Africa. Once I left Africa and arrived in America, I learned the truth, but I was sworn to secrecy."

Fernando was impatient for the truth and said, "Go on, tell us."

Constantine continued, "You see, in truth, I did not survive the beating that my uncle gave me on the day of the fire. I was able to run with the dark-skinned man all the way to the cave on the coast, but the bleeding in my body was so heavy that I died only hours after we arrived. It seems that the dark-skinned man disposed of my body very thoroughly, and it was never discovered by anyone."

"How are you here, then?" Pessoa demanded. "I see a body right here in front of me. And what about the training you received, was that all a lie?"

"No, my friend, everything that I have told you was true to how I remembered it," Constantine said.

"But we talked after you left for America many times. You should have told me!" Pessoa scolded.

Constantine closed his eyes and nodded his head in deference. It was obvious that he had not relished this moment of revelation. "What I was later told was that, after I died, the dark-skinned man gave birth to the self that you speak to now. With his deeply accomplished powers of concentration and creativity he imagined me reborn."

"That is impossible!" Pessoa exclaimed. "One person cannot simply imagine another person into existence. What rubbish are you trying to feed me with?"

Now it was Constantine's turn to scold, "How can you say that, Pessoa? You, who have imagined well over a hundred of your heteronyms into existence. You know that it is possible. You simply didn't imagine that anyone else had the powers that you pride yourself in having."

Pessoa took a deep breath and relaxed and then said, "So, is this dark-skinned man one of the other three master dreamers, then?"

"No, I do not believe so, at least he was not a master at the time that he gave me life. Perhaps he has become one by now. This is all I know; I was told nothing more about my rebirth."

"Told by who?" Pessoa shouted. "Who gave you all this information? Who told you that you died after the fire? Who implied that the dark-skinned man was connected to this boy? Who? Who? Who are you talking about? The old woman? Who is it that you think is equal to me in the art of dreaming?"

Constantine took all of this in stride and continued calmly. "Pessoa, soon after I arrived in America, I was contacted by an old woman. It was she that told me about my death. She said that she had sent the dark-skinned man to make sure that I survived to play my part in some larger plan. When the man was unable to save my physical form, she guided him in the creation of a reborn me; what she calls a 'tulpa."

"Who is she? Who is this woman?" Pessoa was clearly agitated now.

"Her name, Fernando, is Alexandra David-Néel. And she is a master dreamer extraordinaire. In her human birth, she was born outside of Paris in 1868, twenty years before you were born, my friend. She was a precocious child who became a bit of a singing sensation in opera. But her heart was always drawn to matters of spirit and the pursuit of esoteric knowledge and practices. As a young woman, she would travel in search of adventure and enlightenment to the East. Eventually, she would spend fourteen years traveling and studying the most esoteric schools of Tibetan Buddhism. During the years that you were exploring esoteric practices under the tutelage of your aunt Annica, Alexandra was engaged in deep study and practice in India and

Tibet. Of the many magics that she mastered, there was one that involved creating beings of pure thought. These beings were born entirely out of the imagination of a master, and they are called tulpas. Yongden was the name of the dark-skinned man who came to make sure that I saved Tío Marco's life, and survived to play my part in the larger plan. He was Alexandra's closest and most devoted disciple and student, and he was the one who gave me a second birth and created this tulpa form that you see in front of you now. Yongden was an accomplished 'tulpamancer, as one who creates tulpas is called, and a great dreamer as well. But Yongden did not attain full access to the greater realms before his death; although, his work with Alexandra has undoubtedly continued in the dream realms, so, as I said, he may have attained mastery since then."

Fernando had listened to this explanation in silence, but now that Constantine paused his story, Pessoa spoke. "So where is this Parisian? Where is Alexandra the great?" Pessoa said mockingly.

"Stop being such a child, Pessoa," Constantine scolded again. "You should not be so surprised that you were not alone in the art of dreaming. The fact that there is another—"

"A number of others you said," Pessoa reminded.

"Yes, there are others. And their existence does not diminish your accomplishments in the dream realms. Rather than feel slighted, you would do well to rejoice that you have a sister to dream with. I fear that if we knew what lied ahead for us, we would all feel a great deal of relief knowing that we would not have to face the dangers alone," Constantine finished and Pessoa looked humbled. It was a lot to take in all at once. Considering the radical nature of the revelations of the last hour, one could say that Pessoa was taking the news remarkably well. Of course, the four-year-old was completely lost as to the content of the discussion, but he was enjoying immensely being such an important part of an adult conversation.

....

Constantine looked straight into the eyes of the young boy. "Jeff," he said, "I need your older self to come fully forward now. I need the boy to step aside and give up control. It is just like falling asleep. Can you do that?"

The boy nodded.

Somewhere in the recess of the four-year-old's mind, I heard my great-grandfather calling me forward, but I didn't know what to do. I didn't know how to move forward and take control of this little body. I had somehow slipped backward and got stuck.

"Just relax," Constantine said. "You slipped into his unconscious. It is good that I called you forward when I did, if you had fallen much further back, you would have disappeared back to your Earthly body and you'd be sitting with Vicente now instead of us." Constantine continued, "Now, close your eyes and speak. Assume without doubt that your voice will emerge from this body. It is not hard to do. The only thing in your way is the habit of assuming that your voice can only emerge from the body you are most familiar with. If you let go of that assumption, you will find that switching from one body to another is not any more difficult than changing clothes. As soon as you realize that all bodies are but temporary dwellings, then it is easy to switch between them. Just close your eyes and speak."

"Hello, Voovoo," the four-year-old said, then in a tone of great astonishment, the boy continued. "Oh my god, it worked! I am here talking to you now. It is me, my adult self that is talking."

"Very good, Jeff. I knew you could do it," complimented Constantine. "Now I know that you have met with Alexandra on several occasions already. Vicente told me so. She was the woman baking muffins in Paris and she met you again at the farm stand. You remember her, don't you?"

"I have no way of contacting Alexandra. Like you, she came to me in dreams when she wanted to, but I was never able to contact her," Constantine confided, and then he continued, "I haven't seen her in quite some time, but I believe that you are with her now. That is why I needed you here. I need you to take us to her."

"How do I do that?" I asked.

"You have an anchor with her because, in some other dream, you and she are together right now. All you need to do is imagine her in your mind and relax. Don't imagine anything around her, just her, her face maybe, as best as you can remember it. Then you just relax. Slowly you will start to notice things around her. Just let them appear and stay relaxed. If you stay focused on her alone and relax about everything else, the scene around her will appear and gradually stabilize. Once it is stable, you can look around, and then you can imagine us into the scene with you. Just like you did with your friend Colleen once. Imagine us in the next room or behind a door and then open the door and there we will be. Sit here." Constantine motioned for me to sit aside him on the bed.

Constantine turned to face Pessoa. "Are you ready to meet Alexandra, my friend?

"I am ready," Pessoa said softly.

CHAPTER 12

Alexandra's Library

ONE MINUTE I WAS standing with the old woman in the farm stand, and the next I was back in the stone tower. No sooner had I felt her hand touch mine that the scene shifted. It was the oddest transition because I felt no sense of discontinuity. I was suddenly in the stone tower room, and it felt like I had been there for hours even though I remember just having been at the farm. There was no sense of shift.

"Nothing changed, right?" the old woman asked.

"Yes, that's what it feels like. It doesn't feel like I went anywhere even though I am in a completely new place. This is not how it feels in my lucid dreams," I responded.

"Of course. You are a novice dreamer. When one gains mastery of the realms, as I have, and Pessoa also I believe, then you are no longer identified with any particular dream. You are identified with the dreaming itself, and so no matter how scenes shift, and even if you shift from one body to another, you experience only continuity. It is all part of the one dream, and so you move from relative dream worlds smoothly, never forgetting that you are not in any of them, you are in the dream realm. At that point, you are most at home in the dreaming, and no dream feels existentially different from or superior to any other," she explained.

It was then that I realized that I was sitting on the windowsill again just as I had been when I was here before. I looked around at the familiar little room. The oven was still warm, and the muffins were sitting in their tin on top of it exactly where she had left them a moment ago. We had returned to this dream at the precise moment that I had last been here. It felt like exactly the next instant in that dream, and the memory of having been in a farm stand now felt like a dream that I had woken up from and was forgetting.

"The farm feels like a dream now and it is getting further away!" I exclaimed in wonder.

"It *was* a dream, and so, for that matter, is this. The dream you are in always feels like reality when you are in it, and it will feel like a dream the moment you are gone. A master dreamer feels at home in all dreams, and so they all feel real, or you could say that none of them feel real. No particular dream feels real to the master, the dreaming is the only reality. When you liberate yourself into the dream realms, you have liberated yourself from adherence to any particular dream. You are free from seeing any dream as more real than any other. You have come to realize that dreaming itself is the only reality. Everything else is simply appearance." Alexandra was becoming quite animated as she spoke.

"Are you saying that nothing is real except dreaming? What about the dreamer? Is the dreamer real?" I asked.

"To answer that question, we must first agree on what we mean when we say real. If by real we mean something that exists, then the answer is yes. The dreamer is real. But if by real we mean something that is existentially privileged over other things that exist, or even other possibilities that could exist - in other words, something that is more real than all other things - then the answer is no. The dreamer is not real. Who is more real, the aspect of you that is here with me now, or the one that met me at the farm, or the one that is learning about dreaming from Vicente? Is one of those the real you, while the others are just dreams? Do you know why they all feel equally real when you are dreaming them?"

"No," I answered honestly.

"Because they are all real. No dream is more real than any other. That is the radically transformative insight of the dream master. All of the dreams you have lived, and every one that you ever will or could live, are all real. You are not a person having dreams. You are a dream that shifts from one world and one identity to the next. Do you understand? You are not a person. You are a dream!" The old woman was nearly shouting now. "Do you understand?"

I looked at her face. Her eyes were so piercing and deep. It seemed like the lines in the skin around them must have been created from the heat that was generated inside them. She stared straight through me. I felt the energy of her gaze passing through my mind. It was melting my resistance and shining light on the impossible.

"Do you understand?" she asked again.

"Yes!" The word was not spoken by me. It simply emerged out of my mouth. I did not say it. It said itself through me. "Yes!" I repeated more loudly now. "Yes! Yes! Yes! I understand. I see!"

As my mind raced to catch up with what my mouth was saying, a sudden surge of relief washed over me. It was as if every cell in my body had been clenched like a tight fist, and they had all in unison suddenly released. An image of my body with open palms danced through my mind's eye. A vibration of releasing energy passed through me with a tremor. I was shaking all over. Tension that had been trapped in my body since before the day I was born was suddenly relieved. I saw ribbons of colored light passing through my skin. My body was so light now that it floated upward toward the ceiling. I looked down at the old woman from above.

"I see!" I shouted again.

And I really did see now. My mind had finally begun to catch up with what was happening. I saw that everything in a dream is made up of dream stuff. The stone windowsill was made of dream, the muffins were made of dream, my body was made of dream, even my thoughts and feelings were made of dream matter. Dreaming is the only reality. I suddenly thought of my quote/unquote, "real life." It was clear that was a dream too. And my firm conviction that somehow my real life was not a dream, was also part of the dreaming. There was nowhere to go and nothing to see that was not another dream. There is only the dream and nothing else. Even the dreamer is merely a dream of being a dreamer.

"The dream is all there is!" I shouted. "I am that! I am the dream. There is nothing else that I could be!"

The old woman looked up at me with a huge smile on her face. "You have finally been dreamed awake," she said. "Come down here and follow me. I have something to show you."

As soon as the old lady said this, I started to descend. I had willed it to happen, just like I had willed myself to float in the first place. I now saw that the dreaming is controlled using a depth of willfulness that is profoundly subtle. Slight energetic directives, almost too weak to be perceived, guide everything that happens. The slightest intention manifests in the dream, but strong intentions pass through the dream like a hand passes through the air.

Once I was again standing on the ground, the old woman spoke. "My, that was dramatic. I had hoped you would wake up, but I must admit that it happened more easily than I imagined. I guess I will have to give Pessoa and his heteronym, Vicente, some credit, they taught you well. But we do not have time to waste. We must get to the library."

With that, the old woman took my hand and led me out the door into a long circular staircase that curved around a huge stone column. We kept spiraling down the staircase, with the inner column on our left and the outer wall lined with burning candles on our right. We walked down and down and down. We made what felt like twelve full revolutions around the massive inner column. Finally, I saw a big doorway with a heavy wooden door in it at the bottom of the stairs.

"Here it is," said the old woman dramatically as she held the large metal ring that hung from the right side of the door. She slowly pushed the heavy door open. It opened slowly with a loud creak. Even though the old woman was clearly exerting herself strenuously to open the door, I had the feeling that I should allow her to open it without my assistance. Once the door was fully open, I could see that it had opened into a well-lit room. The old woman stood in front of the open door and motioned me forward.

"Come in," she said. "Welcome to my library."

I stepped through the doorway and looked upward into the largest room I had ever seen in my life. It was marvelous, truly marvelous. The room was at least 300 or 400 feet long and about the same wide, but what was truly breathtaking was how high it was. All four walls had balconies full of bookshelves on them. The continuous line of bookshelves on every level was broken periodically by a space that contained a large window. Light from some unseen sun was streaming into the room through the windows on my left. There were at least twenty levels of balcony before I could see the ceiling very high overhead. I had never seen anything like it. I could not even guess how many books were held in this place – certainly hundreds of thousands, if not more.

"Impressive, isn't it?" the old lady asked with her hands on her hips. She was scanning across the impossibly high walls lined with books. I looked back at her and the expression on my face must have implied a question. "Go ahead," she said, "use that staircase." She pointed toward a staircase that led up to the first balcony level of books. The ground floor had no shelves of books. Instead, it was filled with wooden tables. Each table was surrounded by six heavy wooden chairs, and in the center of the table there was a small lamp. I ran to the bottom of the nearest staircase and started up to the first balcony.

I looked at the first shelf of books. They were massive volumes. I looked back at the old woman, and as if she were reading my mind, she said, "Yes, go ahead, open one."

I picked up a massive volume that was so heavy I could hardly lift it. I put it on a small reading table that overlooked the room below. I placed it down carefully, and it landed with a thud, and a plume of dust blew out from between its pages. The cover looked like red leather with complex patters across its surface. I opened the book and saw similar markings throughout. The markings didn't seem to be in rows as I would expect if they were words and phrases from a language I didn't recognize. They looked more like patterns of shapes that seemed to begin in the center of the page and move towards the edges, expanding in size as they went.

"That isn't a language you're likely to recognize," the old woman shouted. "I got that one from one of the non-human dream realms."

"What are all these?" I asked motioning with a sweep of my arm to indicate that I was referring to the books.

"Come down here, and I will explain," she answered.

When I had descended the stairs from the balcony, the old woman and I sat at one of the tables together. "This," she said looking around at all the balconies filled with books, "is the greatest library of spiritual and esoteric knowledge in all of the dream realm. It includes important sacred texts from thousands upon thousands of dream worlds." She then pointed toward the fourth story balcony. "You see the fourth and fifth balconies there?"

"Yes, I see them," I answered.

"Half of the books on those two balconies, the ones on that wall and that wall," she said pointing to two of the walls, "represent all of the spiritual religious traditions in the dream world we call Earth - the one that you knew as the real world."

"Just two half floors?" I said.

"That is a lot of books. Those are huge floors," she defended.

"That is not what I meant," I said, wanting to avoid leaving the wrong impression. "I just meant, if those are all the spiritual books of Earth, then where are all the other books from?"

" Oh, I see," she said. "That is a great question. They come from dream worlds throughout the dream realm, but that will not mean much to you until I explain a bit more about myself."

"Please do," I said.

"My name is Alexandra David-Néel. I was born outside of Paris in 1868. I was an opera singer for a time, and I was good in spite of the fact that I started my career dreadfully late. Singing was not my heart's true passion. Esoteric wisdom and spiritual enlightenment were my only real concerns." She paused at this point and looked at me curiously. "Are you sure you haven't heard of me? I know you are a spiritually minded young man, and I influenced so many people."

"No, I'm sorry. I haven't heard of you before now," I said.

"Never mind," she said brushing my comment aside. "I traveled extensively through Asia and eventually found my way to the forbidden city of Lhasa in Tibet. For fourteen years, I studied and traveled. I took a master from whom I learned the ways of Tibetan Buddhism. My master was the Gomchen of Lachen, and he gave me my religious name, Yeshe Tome, but please, I never use it. Call me Alexandra. My master is the one who taught me the art of dreaming. Once I learned to enter the dream realms, I realized that out there…" she made a wide sweeping motion with her hand, "there are worlds upon worlds, and all of them have discovered different spiritual wisdom and developed esoteric practices. Comparative religion was a driving force for me, and so I became consumed with an exploration of all of the spiritual traditions and mystical paths of the dream realm."

"But after a time, I began to notice something. It was a nearly universal phenomenon. You see the great esoteric wisdom of the realms was all in decline. Everywhere I went, these traditions were being forgotten and sometimes even destroyed. I began to realize that the dream realms as a whole were slowly slipping into a dark age in which the wisdom traditions would be lost. I had already seen this happening on Earth. I lived on Earth in exciting spiritual times. The Russian immigrant, Helena Blavatsky, had established the esoteric tradition of Theosophy, and it was in that tradition that I was initiated into the mystic arts. Later, I was one of the earliest pioneers of Eastern spiritual traditions." Alexandra seemed to be bragging now. "In 1912, I became the first Western woman to be granted an audience with the 13th Dalai Lama, and four years later I entered the Tibetan city of Lhasa incognito because at that time it was still closed to foreigners. Certainly, you've heard of

Alan Watts and Ram Dass, and of course those self-named dharma bums, the Beat poets." I nodded in agreement to show that I was familiar with everyone she had just mentioned. "Well, I inspired them all." This last statement was said triumphantly.

"But let me get back to the point," she said. "I could see on Earth that the growing dominance of a system of science that was based on a purely materialistic assumption about reality was threatening to destroy our planet's mystical traditions. As I traveled the worlds of the dream realm, learning all I could about the esoteric practices to be found there, I realized that something similar was happening everywhere, in every world throughout the dream realm. I did not know why, but the mystical paths were disappearing from the realm. That is when I decided to establish this library, the greatest collection of sacred texts ever amassed in the dream realm. It is here that I intend to preserve as much of the great wisdom as I can, so that it will survive this new dark age and bring light to those that follow. And this is why you are here. You see, I need your help. You have a role to play in this grand attempt to preserve the deepest discoveries of the soul. I realize that you are having to take all of this on faith at this point, but I think I have shown you enough to have earned the benefit of the doubt."

I stood, suddenly released from my rapt attention. I had been mesmerized by her story, and now I was back in my body, looking out over this magnificent library and trying to process all that I had been told. "Why me? Why do I have a part to play in this?" I asked.

"To be honest, that outcome is much more random than you might think. I wish I could say, because you are the one Neo, or that it was foretold in the great scriptures, or something more dramatic. But the truth is much less dramatic. In fact, the details of how it came to be that you have such an important part to play in such a grand endeavor are so mundane and would take so long to explain that I fear I would bore both of us to death in telling it all. It will be much simpler, and more or less accurate, to simply say this. You have such an important part to play in the greatest adventure ever to take place in the dream realm for two reasons. The main reason is because you are willing. You don't know it yet, and believe me you will doubt it many times, but in your deepest heart you are willing, and that alone qualifies you for the job. Again, I wish I could tell you that you were born with special powers or a unique destiny, but the fact is you are willing to do it, and that is enough. The second reason that it is you, and not any one of hundreds of other people who might be willing, is because your great-grandfather died when he was supposed to live."

At that exact moment, a small boy of no more than four or five years old walked in the door that we had walked through about an hour before. He was followed by two men. One very old, the other middle-aged. I immediately recognized that the small boy wearing one-piece pajamas with little football players all over it was me. The other two were my great-grandfather and Fernando Pessoa.

"I see you have finally arrived," Alexandra said, seemingly addressing my great-grandfather. "Mr. Pessoa," she said with a deep bow. "I have been waiting a long time to make your acquaintance."

CHAPTER 13

Alexandra Explains Everything

ALEXANDRA STARTED MOVING CHAIRS away from one of the tables and then motioned to me to help. I jumped to her side and maneuvered enough chairs for all of us to sit on.

"Sit, sit," Alexandra called out. Everyone sat except my four-year-old self, who instead stood in front of one of the big chairs. Alexandra bent forward on her chair and touched the boy on the head. "It is lovely to see you here," she said with a smile.

The boy had not said anything since seeing his older self in the library as he passed through the doorway. Inside his small body there was an insurmountable sense of conflict. It had been difficult enough for the young boy to contend with the appearance of an older aspect of his mind, but now seeing an older aspect of himself physically present in the room had simply stopped his mind. Of course, the conflict was experienced much more severely by the adult in his mind.

One adult aspect of Jeff had come to the front of the young body, a second aspect was standing in an adult body in the room with the young boy. The adult in the young body could move mechanically as directed but was, for all intents and purposes, frozen in disbelief. It is very difficult to describe the feeling of seeing your body separated from you. You see yourself in front of you, making movements that are so deeply familiar to you, but are now being acted out in a body that is not the one you are residing in. You know those movements intimately, and yet they are happening outside of you. You hear your own voice coming out of a body that is yours, but not the one you are in. There is simply no way to absorb that experience.

Noticing the obvious vacancy in the young boy's eyes, Alexandra addressed him, "Jeff, I realize that you are in shock at seeing yourself, but there was no other way to get Connie and Fernando here. I have seen myself in this way only twice before, and I hope never to have that unpleasant experience again. I would not have inflicted it upon you if there had been any other way. If I explain to you how you came to be split, it might help you acclimate to being plural. Years ago, when you were experimenting with lucid dreaming, you came to visit me in the high tower room. I know you remember that." The adult aspect of Jeff nodded with the boy's head. "You eventually woke up from that dream, but I held a part of you back – what we call an aspect. I did that because I knew that I would need to have a part of you that could act as an anchor so that you could bring Constantine and Fernando to me."

At hearing this last statement, Fernando glanced menacingly at Constantine. Pessoa did not like being manipulated, and this was all starting to sound like a plot that had been carried out all around him without his knowing anything about it.

"Stop fussing," Alexandra said to Fernando. "In a moment you will understand why it all had to be this way." Then turning her attention back to the four-year-old body in front of her, she said, "Unfortunately, once such a split is solidified with direct contact, there is no way to reunify the two aspects. In the realm of dreams there will always be two of you, just like there are two of me. I know what it is like to have another aspect of yourself running around," she turned now to face the aspect in the adult body and added, "for both of you. Personally, I try to avoid my other half, and for her part, she seems to try to avoid me, but I don't know how the two of you will work things out. That is up to you. There is no reason that you cannot be friends if you want to be."

The adult aspect of Jeff turned to the young boy and held out his hand. The young boy reached for it, and as their hands touched, a jolt of energetic recognition seemed to jump between their hands. Tears started streaming out of the adult's eyes, and he wrapped his arms around the child. He had never felt so much compassion for himself. He could see himself in the eyes of that child, and he could feel everything that it was to be himself. It was overwhelming and beautiful to see yourself so concretely.

As the two aspects of Jeff hugged each other and sobbed, Constantine gasped loudly, got up from his chair, and sprinted across the room like a much younger man.

What had caused such an eruption of joy was the sight of the dark-skinned man entering the room. Constantine threw himself into the arms of his tulpamancer, and now he was also sobbing.

"Ah," said Alexandra with delight. "That was a reunion I have anticipated for years. It is a very special occasion when any tulpa has the chance to reacquaint with their tulpamancer, but it is especially moving when it has been so long, and when their last meeting was also their first."

Yongden held the sobbing old man and whispered soothing words into his ear. "It is so good to see you, my child. So good to see you again." After a few minutes, Constantine became calm, and the two men walked back to take seats with the others. Alexandra then spent some time explaining to Fernando and Constantine about the library they were sitting in and why she had gathered it. She told the story of the decay of mysticism throughout the dream realm and her desire to revitalize it everywhere. When at last everyone was caught up with what everyone else knew, it was time for her to reveal what no one knew but her.

"Now that you know a little about me and what I have discovered about the declining state of spirituality through-out the dream realm..." Then she turned to Pessoa and added, "You and I have more to talk about in terms of that, my new friend." Pessoa looked pleased with that, and Alexandra repeated her initial sentence. "Now that you know a little about me and what I have discovered about the de-clining state of spirituality throughout the dream realm, I need to explain how we all came to be a part of this ad-venture together. You will see that there is one person that connects all of us, and that person is your aunt Annica, Pessoa," she said turning toward Pessoa.

"Did you know my aunt?" Pessoa questioned.

"Yes, I knew her. And as you know, she was also acquainted with the mystic arts, and she was involved with Theosophy as I was. I met her in Paris in the early 1890's when I was staying at the Theosophical Society headquarters for a time. Annica came to visit and stayed for a few weeks. We became engrossed with each other. She had such an intuitive sense and deep mystical energy. We were only together for a short time, but we loved each other very much. It was during that time that she mentioned you to me." Alexandra looked at Pessoa as she said this. "She told me that her sister had given birth to a spiritually gifted boy only a few years before. She described the intense aura of light around the boy and the depth of his eyes. Now, of course, it is not uncommon for people to mistakenly believe that the children in their families are spiritually gifted, but Annica spoke with such passion about you that I was inclined to be curious. After she left Paris and went back to Lisbon, we maintained contact through letters. A few years later, I received a disturbing letter from her. She had come to believe that her nephew's spiritual gifts had garnered the attention of dark forces and that they were attempting to murder the child. She was beside herself with anxiety and begged me to come to her. I could not let my friend down, so I came and spent a week with her in Lisbon, and I spent one afternoon visiting with you and your mother." Again, she addressed Pessoa directly.

"I do not remember that visit," Pessoa stated.

"I know you don't. We made sure to erase it from your memory. But do not doubt, there was a meeting. I spoke with you and questioned you about your dreams. I could also see a brilliant aura around your head, and the way you spoke of your dreams certainly convinced me that you had a gift. You spoke of a recurring dream involving a man who led an army of demons and monsters. It seemed like a typical child's nightmare, but somehow, I knew it was more than that. There were dark forces attempting to take your life for reasons that I still don't fully understand, but I believe it has to do with the role that you will play in restoring the mystical soul of the dream realm." She paused here for a moment. "As you know, I have been largely in hiding for a long time. My energy has been consumed by collecting these books." She waved her arm to indicate the shelves all around. "And I have done my best to do it in secret. This library is a dream world of its own and well hidden from any other. I have had a few close calls, but until now I have remained safely out of sight."

"That explains how you know me, but you said we were all connected through my aunt. Did Constantine and his great-grandson know aunt Annica?" Pessoa asked.

"On that day that I visited you, your house was being cleaned by a woman who was also named Maria, like your mother. This Maria was not the regular cleaning woman; she was filling in for a sick friend who could not make it. Maria the cleaning woman was your mother Connie," Alexandrea said looking at Constantine, who himself was still staring at Yongden, "and on that particular day, she had needed to bring you with her to work. That was how I met you. And you need not try to remember, because like

Pessoa, all memory of the day has been removed from your mind. When I saw the cleaning woman's child his aura was so bright, I felt as if I had to close my eyes. I had come to see one gifted child and I was meeting two. When I questioned you about your own dreams, I was frightened to discover that you were having the same nightmarish visions of a man leading an army of demons. Whoever was trying to finish Pessoa, was also trying to finish you. There are mysterious forces in creation, both on the side of light and the side of darkness. I could only believe that the coincidence of Constantine being present at the house on the occasion of my only visit to see Pessoa, must have been orchestrated by someone. Annica and I came to believe that we had to act fast. We came up with two simple plans. Constantine would go to live with his uncle in Madeira, and Fernando would go with his mother and her new husband to South Africa. We believed that the two gifted boys would be safer if they were apart and if they were far away from Lisbon. That is what we had thought anyway, but two things got in the way."

"First, I had seen that Connie was going to let his uncle die in a fire, and then he would be sent back to Lisbon where he would surely be killed, so I sent Yongden to him to make sure that his uncle survived so that he could stay in Madeira. But then that evil man…" then to herself she said, "Oh, how I hate that man… managed to kill little Connie in his drunken rage." Realizing suddenly that Connie was one of the people in the room she turned to him. "I am so sorry Connie. We would never have sent you to that man if there had been another way."

Constantine nodded understandingly.

"Once you had died, I instructed Yongden to make a tulpa from your memory. As a tulpa, you could not do the work that the human Constantine was destined to do, but you could still instruct Fernando and pass on the wisdom of dreaming. Luckily, you were born." Now she turned toward the adult aspect of Jeff. "You had inherited the gift that your great-grandfather had had, and he instructed you and helped develop it while you were young. So, the plan was saved, and Connie was even able to arrange that you receive the best possible instruction from Fernando and Vicente." Fernando smiled at the compliment.

"The second thing that went wrong, or I should say, is going wrong right now, is that a rogue dreamer, and I think I know who it is, has gone to the ship that originally carried Pessoa and Constantine to South Africa. She intends to kill you both there and foil all the work we've done. I will soon have to leave you all so that I can rectify that situation."

"You can't leave yet." Pessoa insisted. "I have many more questions."

"Yes, I am sure you do, and all of your questions will be answered in time. Right now, I have just enough time to explain a few important things in brief." She paused and adjusted herself in her chair before continuing.

"In some ways you were right all along my friend, there are certain elemental forces that do not want humans to gain free access to the dream realms. You see these non-human agents have been traveling unchallenged through the realms for a long time. They have manipulated human beings through our dreams and nightmares, and even our daydreams and fantasies, and they do not want humans becoming dream masters. Some of these elemental forces are trying to hide esoteric wisdom. As you know Pessoa, many of these esoteric practices hold the key to dreaming and they want to be sure that humans do not find it. Originally, they only needed to hide the esoteric practices of the Earth, but once they discovered that I had gained mastery of dreaming, they knew that I would discover more secrets and train more humans to travel the dream worlds of the realm. When I realized that they planned to kill me, I went into hiding. Then they realized that I had discovered the two gifted boys that they knew they would need to kill as well, and since I was in hiding, they accelerated their plans to destroy the esoteric wisdom of the realm before I could preserve much of it. They have been running around the worlds of the dream realm destroying the wisdom as fast I have been trying to preserve it. I have had a few close run-ins with them, but so far, I have managed to stay alive and well. We will never know how much of the great wisdom they have destroyed, but I have saved a great deal of it."

Pessoa looked at the old woman in front of him with newfound respect. His prideful animosity had melted away as he saw what a great service she was doing on behalf of humanity. "We all owe you a great deal of gratitude." He said slowly. "It seems you have saved my life, and in at least a sense Connie's life as well. I see now why you said that I was partly right. I was right to believe that the Elementals wanted to block humanity from entering the dream realms. But I was wrong in thinking that the necessary course of action was to destroy them. I see now that we must preserve the esoteric traditions because in their wisdom lies humanity's access to the dream worlds of the realm."

"Yes Pessoa." Alexandra said. "We cannot destroy the Elementals. We must preserve the wisdom, and perhaps in time humans and Elementals can learn to live in harmony. But I do not have time to speak more of this. You and I have many more conversations ahead I promise you, but there is one more thing that I must do here before I make my leave."

Now Alexandra turned to the adult aspect of Jeff. "I am sorry this had to get so complex. I needed to use you as an anchor to guide your 4-year-old self to me so that Constantine and Pessoa could find their way here. And at the same time, Pessoa sent another aspect of you to the ship heading to South Africa to save Connie and his own boyhood-self there. This unfortunately means that you have been split now into four aspects. One is the adult aspect that I am speaking to now. Then there is the four-year-old standing here," She turned toward the boy in pajamas. "and of course, there is another adult aspect of you inside that body as well. The fourth aspect is now onboard the ship heading for South Africa."

"Before I go, I must clean up this mess. First, my child," she said looking down at the boy in pajamas. "you must go to sleep." She put her hand on the boy's forehead and he immediately laid down on the floor and fell fast asleep. "That is simple enough. When the child wakes up, he will not remember much, if any, of this dream. And now that the boy is back to sleep, the adult aspect of you has now also returned to his session with Vicente; the one from which he merged with his four-year-old self. You will remember some aspects of this dream, those that I allow you to, and you will report them faithfully to Vicente. The information you pass on will cause Pessoa to conclude that you and Vicente must go to the ship bound for South Africa to save Connie and Pessoa as boys. Pessoa wisely chose not to accompany you because he feared that complications might arise if he were to meet his boyhood self. That was a very astute choice." She nodded approvingly toward Pessoa. "As for the aspect of you that is onboard the ship, assuming I am successful in averting disaster there, and all goes as well as possible, that aspect will return to the session with Vicente from which they made the journey to the ship. You, the aspect here with us will then be the primary aspect. You will have the greatest knowledge of all that has happened, and the others will become part of your memories. All back to normal." She seemed very pleased with herself.

"But now," she said abruptly as if she had realized it was getting late. "I must go to the ship myself and stop a terrible thing that is about to happen there. I am tempted to take Yongden with me, but I believe it is best if I go alone. Pessoa and Connie must wait here because there are already other versions of you onboard that ship, and we have had enough plurality exposure for one day. No need to worry, from your point of view this will just take a moment."

Saying this Alexandra walked toward and then through the same door that she and Jeff had entered the library through in the first place. And it was only a moment later when she walked back through the door. Pessoa's first thought was that she had forgotten something and had come back for it, but then he saw that she was soaking wet and he realized that she was actually returning from whatever adventure had awaited her on the ship.

"Are you alright?" Pessoa asked as the three men rushed toward her. Alexandra stumbled into the library and waved the men away.

"Yes, I am alright. Everything is alright for now. The disaster was averted, but not without cost. I will tell you the whole story."

Then a second man walked in behind her. He wore a suit and he was covered in an oozing slime.

CHAPTER 14

The Lady in the Red Dress

THE LADY IN THE red dress stood up from the bed and was hovering over the third mate who was now awkwardly leaning halfway up under his blanket wearing a nightshirt.

"Get up!" she commanded. "We are going to have to see the captain now. I hadn't wanted to get him involved. If only you had just stuck to the agreement, but now we will have to make this a huge spectacle. It is always tempting when working in the subtle art of unconscious manipulation to compromise and work with idiots." Edwards felt vaguely insulted as she continued. "Influencing someone who is intelligent and sensitive is very difficult; it takes years. There is always the temptation to work with a dullard like you. The process is so fast that way. You just provide something that the person could never achieve on their own, like a third mate assignment, or being the captain of a ship, and the person will be yours for life. Unfortunately, their loyalty to your will is always limited by their ability to effectively enact it. What is the use of having a loyal servant like you, who cannot follow through on a simple plan? Get up! And get dressed. We have to go now."

When the captain opened the door and saw the lady in the red dress his mouth dropped open. She had not come to see him for so long that he had hoped she might never return. And his surprise was amplified by seeing his third mate, supposedly loyal to him, standing behind her.

"Hello captain. You look surprised to see me." Said the lady in the red dress.

"I was not expecting you, but your ladyship is always welcome to call on me." Answered the captain.

"Of course, I am." She responded. "You are also surprised to see your third mate with me. Do you think even he is stupid enough to get into a fight on shore during his very first assignment? I admit, it didn't take much to get him started, but still, without my influence he would never have caused all that trouble. Unfortunately, he had something he needed to do for me, and he has failed and now I am going to have to get you involved to finish the job. Unfortunately, we are going to have to make a public event out of all this – exactly what I had hoped to avoid. It is not a complicated affair. There is a young stowaway on your ship. He is hiding with that woman Maria and her young son, Fernando."

"A stowaway!" the captain said out loud. "How do I not know about this?" he added looking at Edwards.

"Don't get all worked up. It was all my doing. Now we are going to have to go to Maria's cabin and demand the boy. She will not want to give him up. She knows how important he is. So, you are going to have to bring some men and take the boy. Then you must throw him overboard. In the scuffle, Edwards is going to make sure that the young Fernando goes overboard as well." She looked back and forth at the two men. "Do you think you two can handle this?"

The two men looked at each other, both feeling entirely trapped. This woman somehow had power over them. Neither of them wanted to do what she asked, and at the same time both of them knew that they would. They did not have the power to choose otherwise and they didn't understand why not. Instead of objecting in any way, both men simply nodded in agreement.

"Good, now let's go get them." The lady in the red dress started walking toward Maria's cabin. Hearing no footsteps following her, she stopped and turned toward the two men. "Come!"

They started walking. The captain was dressed impeccably in his uniform and the third mate was still trying to tuck his shirt into his trouser. Edwards wondered if the captain actually slept in his uniform, or if he did not sleep at all.

This time it was the captain who knocked on Maria's door. There was the sound of scrambling on the other side of the door and then the sound of a voice. "Who's there." Said a woman's voice.

"It is me Maria, the captain. I am sorry to visit you so late, but there is a matter of great urgency that we must discuss."

"What is it about?" said Maria

"The extra boy you have with you. Edwards is here with me and I know all about the young stowaway." The captain said.

"You don't need to worry about the boy. He will be fine with us. I will pay for his transport. He is not your concern anymore. Goodnight sir." Maria said definitively.

"Please mam, do not make me breakdown this door to retrieve the boy. I will not allow for stowaways on board my ship. It sets a bad example. If ships allowed stowaways, there would be dozens of them on every voyage." The captain pounded hard on the door. "Mam, I must insist that you let me in. Now!"

"Break the door in if you must, but I am not opening it." Maria said defiantly.

"What should we do?" the captain asked the lady in the red dress. "If we bang down the door it will affect all of the other passengers."

"Yes, well that is not my concern. It was Edwards here that gave the boy to her in the first place. He is the cause of this unfortunate situation." She looked at the captain expectantly.

"Go get a battering ram." The captain ordered and Edwards ran off, a few minutes later he reappeared with a long wooden pole with three handles on it. He held the pole toward the captain and both men held firm to one of the handles.

"Back up Maria, we are coming in now." The captain warned and then the two men took ten steps back and then on a count of three ran forward crashing into the door. The door banged open and Maria screamed loudly.

Once inside, the lady in the red dress grabbed Maria by the wrists and pulled her into a corner of the room. "Hello Maria. You do not know me, but I know all about you and your sister Annica. You have caused a great deal of trouble meddling in affairs of which you have no real understanding. You were trying to hide these two boys from me, but I knew what you were doing. It was a fairly simple matter to manipulate that drunk Marco and make sure that the boy became so distressed that he would find his way to this vessel. You see I wanted your son and the boy together so that I could dispose of both of them and you all at once. And doing it out here at sea will mean that all I need to do later is sink this vessel and no one will ever know what happened. After that I will pay my old friend Annica a visit."

"How could you destroy this vessel and everyone on board?" Maria implored.

"Human life is one of the most expendable items in all the realm. Even you must know by now how many lifetimes we live. Most of them utterly useless and of no consequence. Moving a person from one lifetime to the next is almost never a disservice. It simply speeds them along on the trajectory of what was inevitable anyway."

"You are wrong, you witch!" Maria exclaimed. "Every human birth has the potential to act as the entryway into the dream realm. Anyone at any time could find their way to the wider reality and roam freely as you do. You, and others like you, are blocking humanity's path to the greater realms. You hold us in one drastically limited universe of possibility and then justify doing whatever you want with us by claiming that our lives are meaningless because we live in a universe of such limited possibility."

"Imagine two buckets, both full of maggots." The lady in the red dress explained. "You reach your hand into one bucket and pull out a handful of them. You reach your other hand into the other bucket and pull out a handful from there. Now you exchange the handfuls so that the maggots that came from one bucket end up in the other. You have exchanged hundreds, maybe thousands of them, but there is no appreciable difference. You still have two buckets full of maggots. All the people on this ship will go somewhere else, and it is just as likely as not that their next life will be better than this one."

"You Elementals are so callous. Your access to the greater realms should make you more compassionate, but instead you become hardened to the suffering you cause."

"Unfortunately, we do not have time to continue this conversation any longer. But simply as a matter of interest, I am not an Elemental. You humans make up a word and then use it to describe all non-human entities. And because you only have one word to describe them all, you assume we are all one thing. You know so very little about what exists."

With this she turned to face the bedroom door, and then, to end the conversation she said, "Say what you will, it will change nothing. You and the boys will die here to-night, and once that is confirmed everyone else on board will die of a terrible accident at sea."

As the two women spoke in the corner of the room, the third mate and his captain ran into the bedroom finding the two boys huddled together behind the big bed. The captain grabbed Fernando and his third mate grabbed the stowaway.

"We have them." The captain declared as he and his third mate dragged the two young boys into the room.

CHAPTER 15

The Captain and His Third Mate Discover Hope

BY THE TIME THEY arrived on the deck at the stern of the boat, the morning sun was just becoming visible. The ocean was a little rough and the ship was swaying up and down. There were high clouds in the sky, but they cleared near to the horizon, so it was a beautiful morning. As they approached the railing at the edge of the deck you could see the trail of foam left behind by the moving ship. Passengers were generally not allowed on the aft end of the ship and so Fernando and his mother, and of course also Connie, were seeing this view for the first time.

Maria had walked from her cabin to the stern of the ship in silence, matching the stride of the woman in the red dress, step by step. In her mind she was trying to formulate a plan to end this nightmare. Perhaps she thought, she could reason with the captain. There was certainly nowhere to run, but if she could garner enough support from other passengers perhaps the captain would feel pressured to stop.

She knew that there was no plan that would succeed even if her mind could not help but attempt to formulate one. The woman was very powerful, and the two men were obviously completely under her influence. She claimed not to be an Elemental, but she spoke like one and acted like one. Whoever or whatever she was, she was in control and she would not be easy to deal with. Maria was going to let this play out a bit until an opportunity arose for some kind of escape.

At last, the small party arrived at the very rear of the ship. The sound of the engine was a roar and the spray from the ocean was covering them with mist. The sea had become rougher and they were bobbing up and down with the waves. Upon reaching the stern of the ship, the two men turned toward the lady in the red dress. They looked at her as if pleading to be allowed not to do what they both knew she wanted. Neither of them would ever have thrown anyone overboard, never mind two young boys and one of their mothers.

They simply did not know how to stop what was about to happen. It wasn't as though they felt, in some material, way controlled. They both felt fully in control of their bodies. It was something else. They both knew what was going to happen. In fact, they could see it all happening in their minds in meticulous detail. Edwards saw how he would through the stowaway off in one mighty heave. He could see the boy hit the water, float for a moment and then get pulled under by the force of the propellor. Then he saw how the captain did the same with Fernando. He saw how they would both hesitate when it came to the mother, but it didn't matter because she would jump overboard in a useless attempt to save her son's life.

Both Edwards and the captain could see it all - exactly what was going to happen in every detail. They also knew that they didn't have to go through with any of it. They knew that they had the power to resist and not do these terrible things. They also knew that they would not resist. They would do it. Not because they wanted to, or because they chose to. They would do it because it was destined to happen that way. You are always free to choose against your destiny. It just never happens that way. Both men, despite their reservations, felt trapped by inevitability. They could feel the mysterious momentum of the future that would carry them like an ocean current.

Edwards felt his body tense. He realized that this was the moment when he would throw the stowaway overboard. He looked at the boy and he could see that somehow the boy knew it too. Edwards could see in the boy's eyes the silent knowing that this was the end. It was so sad to see such heaviness in the boy. Edwards wished with all his heart not to do what he was about to do, but he knew he would.

"Well, well, well." Came the sound of a voice above the noise of the engine. "What is going on here?" Maria had never been so happy to hear anyone before. She turned and saw two men in odd dress. She immediately felt the relief of being saved, although even a moment's thought might have convinced her that the appearance of these two strangers only delayed the inevitable.

"Get them!" the lady in the red dress shouted and the captain and third mate ran at the intruders, in spite of the fact that they were just as relieved to see them as Maria had been.

One of the men looked at the other and said, "Remember, just like I told you, don't move."

The captain and the third mate ran at the two men in odd clothes as if to tackle them, but soon they found that they had run straight through them. They ran through the bodies as if they were made of sea mist. Edwards had run so hard that he banged into the large pipe that had been behind the men. He saw bright lights dancing around the edges of his vision and then he fell hard to the floor.

The lady with the red dress looked at these two men. "So, you are dreamers. That will not stop me, but I am curious, who are you."

"My name is Vicente Guedes, and my associate is Jeff Carreira. And we are both here at the request of Fernando Pessoa." Vicente looked triumphant at mentioning Pessoa's name.

"This boy requested your presence." The lady said pointing to the young Pessoa.

"Not as a boy, but as a man, as a master dreamer. Pessoa taught me to dream and he asked me to come where he could not, to stop you." Vicente said.

"You will fail, I am sure you can feel that." Said the lady.

"No, in fact I am beginning to feel a shift in the destiny here, and I am sure that you can feel that." Vicente said with confidence.

The lady turned to her two subjects. "Throw them overboard, now" she shouted, but the two men hesitated. The dreadful sense that all of this was inevitable was shifting. They began to have hope that perhaps another outcome was possible. The sense of hope, small that it was, allowed them to defy the order. To hesitate.

"What are you doing?" The lady demanded. "Throw them overboard, now!" Still the two men did not move. The captain and the third mate had discovered hope. For the first time in their lives, they were hopeful; hopeful that another way was possible, hopeful that they were not prisoners of fate, hopeful that they could create positive change. They were experiencing the most important human attribute. Hope, the sense of even the slimmest possibility of positive difference, is what makes being human so precious. It is what so many non-human entities long for. When it goes wrong, when humans mistakenly see negative change as positive, this same sense of hope becomes the cause of so many problems because it drives the wicked equally as the righteous. With their newfound hope, the captain and the third mate resisted their dark destiny and, as they saw themselves resist, their sense of hope multiplied.

The greatest mystical secret is the knowledge that responding to our sense of hope generates greater hope. Our own acts to create a new and positive future strengthen our belief in our ability to do so. By acting upon our own hopeful inclinations, we generate greater and greater power within ourselves. The captain and the third mate were feeling that power now. They were beginning to realize that no one was going to die today, and that realization strengthened their resolve.

"You fools!" shouted the lady, "Do you have any idea what you are resisting?"

But it was no use. The spell had been broken in them. Someone was applying a positive influence on them. The lady did not believe it could be Vicente, he did not seem powerful enough, and it certainly could not be Carreira, he seemed to have almost no idea what he was involved with. It must be Pessoa that was exerting this influence. Even though he dared not come into a realm that already included another aspect of him, he might be working through Vicente to exert influence over the buffoons. But why had he sent Carreira? She could see in that man's eyes that he had no idea at all what was happening. He was so confused. They had brought him into this too quickly. He was not integrated here. He was very vulnerable to influence. Pessoa had made a mistake. It was a stupid mistake. He did not need Carreira's aspect here, it made no sense to bring him. Perhaps he had other reasons of his own, but she knew that it would prove a fatal mistake.

Jeff, or rather this aspect of Jeff, felt a growing sense of doom. He felt invisible tentacles wrapping around his arms and legs. They were the invisible ties of destiny – a dark destiny that he wanted with all his heart to avoid, but that he knew he would not. It was not a loss of free will that he felt. It was the loss of all sense of hope. He knew what he was about to do, and he hated it. He would first throw his own great-grandfather overboard and then Pessoa. After that Maria would jump in and follow her son. The history would be altered, but the destiny would remain the same.

"Yes!" Shouted the lady. "Do it now!"

...

In a new temporary dreamscape, Alexandra and Pessoa sat in a café in the small town of Caminha in northern Portugal. They had been there for some time creating a plan. They knew that they must join forces because neither of them on their own was likely to prevail.

"You must hold off the two seamen." Alexandra said to Pessoa. "You must instill enough hope to embolden them to resist her influence."

"But surely she will simply influence Jeff. He is too strong for me to influence and too weak to resist. He is in the most vulnerable possible place. I should never have brought him. It makes no sense. He was not needed; it was much too dangerous for a training mission. I don't know what I was thinking." With these last words Pessoa stopped speaking. "It was you. You influenced me to send him. What have you done? Why did you put him in harm's way? I fear that you have made a grave mistake."

"It was the only way my friend. It may not work, but there was no other way. We will both see in a moment if my plan has worked. We must try. I cannot explain more now. If I do not go now, all will be lost. Pessoa hold the two men back. Give them hope. You must." Alexandra got up and behind her a circular hole opened in the dreamscape. On the other side of the opening, Pessoa could see the deck of a ship. He was tempted to run and join her, but that was not where he felt hope.

"I will give them hope so they may resist, and I will hope that soon we will be reunited in victory." Pessoa said.

Alexandra stepped through the opening and behind her it closed leaving just the stone fountain in the middle of the square and the cloudy sky above.

CHAPTER 16

Beyond the Wall of Fear

"NO JEFF! YOU DO not have to do this!" Alexandra called out as she stepped onto the deck of the ship.

"You!" shouted the lady. "I should have guessed that it would be you."

"Yes, it has been a long time. Did you think I was gone for good?" asked Alexandra.

Jeff recognized that this was the old lady who had been baking cookies in the tower. He knew her and he trusted her. That trust was enough to allow him to resist the dark destiny that had gripped him only a moment before.

"You know this woman?" asked Vicente, directing his question at the old lady he and Pessoa had been preoccupied with for so long, but was only now finally meeting. "You know her?" he repeated.

"Of course, she knows me." Said the lady in the red dress. "She created me. I am her tulpa. She never even gave me the dignity of a name and so I have never taken one." Then the lady turned toward Alexandra. "You of all people cannot stop me. I am an Independent now, and according to spiritual law you cannot harm me, nor influence another to harm me. In all the realms, you are the one person that I am completely protected from."

"It was a mistake for me to leave you alone for so long in the realms. I was more ignorant then. I did not realize what I was doing. I am truly sorry for that. I did not know the pain I was causing you." Alexandra admitted.

"You should have known. Tulpas need to be with their tulpamancers. The fear and insecurity of being apart is unbearable. You left me out doing your bidding for so long. I did not want to live, but I could not end my existence. I was so lost in the world, forgotten and forsaken by the one who had created me. Then I started to feel angry. Angry with you. Angry at being dependent on you. I wanted to be free. It took a long time and great effort, but I liberated myself from you. I became independent and I found others. Lost tulpas who had been forgotten by those that created them. I helped them to become free. There are many of us now and we do not want to go back. We want to live free and we will protect our freedom with all of our power. You cannot stop us." The lady in red stopped speaking and waited for a response. This was a moment she had imagined for a long time. The moment of confrontation when she would finally be able to tell Alexandra how she felt and what she had accomplished.

Alexandra looked down toward the deck. She was visibly shaken. "It was wrong of me. I always thought that there were reasons that I could not go back for you. There was always one more thing that had to be done first. There were so many reasons, but there was no excuse. I should not have left you alone. You have every right to be infuriated with me, but please do not take out your anger on those that had nothing to do with it."

"As far as I am concerned, the entire human race is at fault. As soon as you gain power of the realms, you start manufacturing other beings to use as your servants and when they are no longer of use, you simply set them adrift. You did not do anything that any other human would do. Look at Pessoa, how many heteronyms did he create and forget. Yes, he has his favorites, Vicente here and Bernardo Soares, Ricardo Reis, Alberto Cairo, and Alvaro de Campos. To those and a few others he is loyal, but there are so many adrift. Forgotten and alone. I have found many of them and believe Pessoa has a great deal to answer for. You are all the same."

The Sun was now higher in the sky, but it was largely covered over by clouds. There was a strong wind that was blowing a great deal of spray from the ocean over the deck. Everyone was getting soaked.

"No, you are wrong." Alexandra interjected. "We are new to the realms, and there is no one to teach us – and worse, someone is trying to block all of the esoteric knowledge, so we are having to move through the realms in darkness and ignorance. I am so sorry I hurt you, I will do anything to make up for it. Please tell me that you will work with me and let these boys go and we can create a better world for humans and independent tulpas alike. Please let's work together."

The lady began to feel a very uncomfortable feeling. It was hope. A small bubble of hope growing in her belly. Perhaps there was a different way. Perhaps humans and Independents could work together. "No!" she shouted, "Not again. I will not be fooled again," and with that she ran toward the stowaway. "I will do this myself!"

As soon as she saw the lady in the red dress turn toward the young stowaway, Alexandra turned toward Jeff. "This will be difficult, but you need to grab her. It is the only way. We will come back for you. I am sorry. This was the only way."

Jeff heard Alexandra's words and he knew he must grab the lady in the red dress. He took just two steps and grabbed her around the waist. The lady was so surprised she did nothing for a moment, and a moment was all Alexandra needed. She reached under her coat and pulled out a small round hand mirror. She held it up toward Jeff's face and shouted. "Jeff, look here!"

It all happened so fast. Grabbing the woman and hearing Alexandra's command. Jeff was such a novice to the realms, his instinct to follow the direct order of the older woman was stronger than the instinct to avoid looking in a mirror at all costs. Anyone with any experience in the realm would have immediately averted their gaze at the first sign of a mirror. Jeff simply did not realize the danger of what he was about to do. This is why he was needed.

Jeff turned his head, and he began to realize that he was turning to face into a mirror, but he had no real idea what was going to result from that simple action. Before he had even registered what had happened, he heard the screams in his head. At first there was nothing in the mirror. Just a reflection of the sea behind him. He was not being reflected at all. Then he started to feel horrible movements in his stomach, all through his body in fact. There was something inside him, many things. He felt them moving and every second he looked into the mirror they seemed to get more agitated inside him. He wanted to look away, but he could not. It was as if his gaze was riveted to the mirror. As the horrible squiggling movements in his body increased, he opened his mouth in a loud scream from the pain he felt. The scream was not his though. The pain was not his either. Both were coming from all those things inside his body.

With his mouth now open he saw something in the mirror. It was not his face, but it was the round opening of his mouth. And inside that opening he did not see teeth and tongue. Instead, he saw horrible creatures. Some with wings, some with claws, still others with fangs. None of them looked like anything he had ever seen before. Some were covered with scales and slime, others with fur or simply leathery rough skin. They were all wailing loudly and trying to escape. These were the creatures that he felt inside him. He recognized the sound. He had heard it in his dream when he had tried to look into a mirror in the bathroom. He felt the same wall of fear he had felt then.

The lady in red was terrified. She had no idea what was happening and suddenly she looked up toward the sky and screamed. Up in the air, fifty feet above the boat, a hole had opened in the sky. The hole was in the shape of a mouth exactly as Jeff was seeing in the mirror. Inside the hole everyone could see the same assortment of creatures that Jeff was seeing in the mirror. It was a passageway to some other realm, a nightmare realm.

Suddenly, Jeff felt a strong tug at his back. He looked at Alexandra with placid resignation. He knew what was about to happen.

"Hold on to her. Make sure she comes with you. We will come back for you – for both of you. There was no other way." Alexandra now looked at the lady in the red dress with tears in her eyes.

"I am so sorry." Alexandra said sobbing.

That was the last thing Jeff heard before his feet left the ground. He was sucked upward very quickly and disappeared into the nightmare hole above, which immediately started to close and disappear as soon as he and the lady were inside. But before the gaping mouth in the sky had fully closed, another man fell out of the hole and onto the deck. The man landed with a wet thud. He was wearing a dark suit and was covered with an oozing slime. He looked up and his face was white as if all the blood had been drained from his body. "Thank you." He said feebly. "Thank you."

CHAPTER 17

H. P. Lovecraft Has Arrived

ALEXANDRA HAD TAKEN SOME time to tell the whole story of what had happened on the deck of the ship, and how the aspect of Jeff that had been there had been sucked into the nightmare realm along with the lady in the red dress. During the entire recounting of the story, she never once mentioned the man sitting next to her. The one who was covered in slime. As for his part, the slimy man simply sat in silence staring at the floor. Now that Alexandra had finished telling the story, she looked at the man sitting next to her.

"As I am sure you have by now guessed, this is the man that fell out of the hole in the sky as Jeff and the lady were sucked into it. He has not spoken since the incident except to say thank you. I believe I know who he is, but I will allow him to introduce himself." Alexandra stopped there giving the man time to speak.

The man looked around at each of the other faces in the room. He used his sleeve to wipe some of the strange material from his face and said, "Hello. My name is Howard Phillips Lovecraft, but you might know me better by my pen name, H.P. Lovecraft."

"Lovecraft!" Pessoa exclaimed. "Is it truly you? I had heard rumors, but I never could confirm them. So, you must be another of the great human dreamers that I have been hearing about."

"I am H. P. Lovecraft. That much is true, but as far as being a great dreamer, I am not sure about that. I created nightmare realms in my dreams that were so vivid and convincing that I got lost in them myself. I have been in there, terrified, for so long. If that makes me a great dreamer than I say that I would rather not be one." Lovecraft finished his statement and fell back into silence, until he said, "I do have one question, if I may?"

"Yes, please ask." Said Alexandra who had presumed the question was being addressed to her.

"How did you know that getting that man to look into the mirror would open up the nightmare realm?"

"I had read things. They were not conclusive and somewhat sketchy, but I had read them in enough places that I was able to piece together that having a human dreamer look into a mirror would open up a nightmare realm and suck them into it. I guessed that by holding onto the lady in red, Jeff would be able to take her with him. It was the only way I could think of to contain her." Alexandra looked down sadly, then she added, "We must go back for them. You know that? And you Lovecraft, we will need you to guide us."

Lovecraft did not want to return to that place ever, but he also did not want anyone else to be trapped there on his account. He knew he would return to release the others. It had the unavoidable feeling of destiny. "I will guide you to save the others." He said.

"Thank you." Alexandra responded to Lovecraft. Then turning to the others in the room she said, "Our entire quest lies ahead of us. If the lady in red had been successful in destroying the boys on that ship, we would not have been completely stopped, after all one of you is now a tulpa anyway, and the other is a dream master who exists independent of any of his aspects, but we would have been severely hampered in our efforts, perhaps irrevocably so."

No one had spoken during Alexandra's explanation of events onboard the ship, but now Pessoa spoke.

"Alexandra, you have proven yourself a master dreamer beyond any doubt, and you certainly possess more intimate knowledge of the ways of the realms than I, yet I believe that we all need more information about the adventures ahead if we are going to join you as comrades in this endeavor. I have been thinking while you spoke, and I believe I have pieced together the broad strokes of the quest."

"As you have already said the mystical arts and esoteric knowledge are being deliberately vanquished from all of the realms. I still believe that this is the work of the Elementals who wish to hide from humanity the accessing practices of dreaming. Currently, the Elementals enjoy free and unchallenged dominance of the realms beyond waking and they have no intention of granting humanity similar access."

"Now I have also learned of a second class of non-human beings, tulpas, and I discover that I have, without fully realizing the implications of what I was doing, created and abandoned a number of these. It seems that at least some of these independent tulpas also have a vendetta against humanity, or at the very least with those that spawned and then abandoned them. What I do not fully understand is what our mission is in the midst of all this."

Pessoa finished and Alexandra addressed everyone. "You are correct in all that you have said. I dedicated my Earthly life to the spread of esoteric wisdom and real magic. I saw in my mind's eye a possibility of a spiritually advanced humanity. Initially, when I realized that the esoteric and mystical knowledge was being lost, I thought only to preserve it. Then I began to realize that it was not just being lost, it was actually being deliberately hidden. Yes, I believe that is in part due to Elemental forces that want to keep the knowledge all to themselves, but I suspect there is more than that going on. You see, the Elementals that we are most familiar with, the non-incarnate beings that were liberated from foundational human elements during our species' earliest history, are themselves just the animation of raw emotional content. In those early days of humanity, some emotions were felt so strongly by so many that the emotions themselves gained a kind of independent existence. So, as you have said many times Pessoa, they were born out of humanity, but they were never, strictly speaking, human."

"But there is another class of Elemental that I have read about in some of the sacred texts of the realms. These are called Upari Elementals, most often simply called Upari. These were not born of human emotion. The Uparis are higher-dimensional beings. They exist in dimensions beyond even the dream realms, and only occasionally pass through the realms. The last time a Upari passed through our realms was during what has come to be known as the Axial Age of humanity. You see, the Upari that passed through the realms at that time is perceived by humans and Elementals alike as either a god, or a deep spiritual energy of love and wisdom, which is in effect the same thing."

"The term Axial age was coined by the philosopher Karl Jaspers in 1949, and he used the phrase to denote a period of time, in this case spanning hundreds of years, when human consciousness shifted as if it were pivoting on an axis. The first Axial Age generated a vast revolution in thinking that resulted in the establishment of countless religious and philosophical movements. The rise of Platonism in Greece that would dramatically influence the subsequent formation of Christianity, happened at this time. The Hundred Schools of Thought in China, that included both Confucianism and Taoism, were also products of the Axial Age. Zoroastrianism, Jainism, Buddhism, and the emergence of the Jewish prophets were also part of this pivotal time. From this perspective, the realms are merely a reflection of this one superbeing."

"I believe that a second Upari is coming. In fact, the leading edge of its being may already have penetrated the outer edges of the realms. As it passes through our dimensions, we will undergo an unimaginable shift. It is possible that the disappearance of great mystical wisdom, most, if not all, of which was a product of the last Axial Age, may be part of the preparation for the arrival of the next Upari."

"This second coming is inevitable, and I believe it could be a glorious rebirth for all of humanity and indeed, all of the beings in all of the realms. I also fear that it could mean our destruction. Strictly speaking, Uparis are neither good nor evil. Their scope of being and motives are so much vaster than our realms, they have no knowledge of us. They pass through our worlds the way we pass through molecules of air, having no idea of the massive disruptions we cause. "

"It is within our power to make that disruption a positive one. What we can learn from the great mystical traditions of the realms will be crucial as we navigate through a new Axial Age in the most beneficial way possible. I do not know what such a small group of dreamers can do to midwife a multi-dimensional rebirth, but I for one am dedicated to doing whatever I can."

Alexandra had finished her speech. She sat back. Pessoa looked at her. Connie sat near Yongden, his tulpamancer, and nodded his agreement. Now that he had been reunited with Yongden, he would not leave his side. Yongden's loyalty to Alexandra was no less unshakeable than that of a tulpa to his tulpamancer; he would go wherever she did.

Pessoa spoke again. "This is certainly the great purpose which I have always known that I was born for. I am dedicating myself to this with all of my heart, mind, body and soul."

Jeff spoke next. His voice was quiet and his words emerged slowly from his mouth. "I probably understand this less than any of you, but I can't go back, I cannot return to the life I was living before. Now that I have seen all of this," Jeff waved his arms to indicate the massive stockpile of books all around, "I must see this through to the end. I guess my biggest concern is that I will not be of any real help, but it feels like destiny that I am a part of this."

"It is indeed." Alexandra said, "Then we are decided, and the first course of action will be to rescue your other aspect and my first tulpa from Lovecraft's dream realm. After that my friend," Alexandra said looking at Lovecraft, "you will be free to do what you please, any debt you have to me will be paid in full. Of course, I hope that you will join us, but that will be up to you at the time."

"I am ready to reenter the nightmare realm, and after that we shall see." Lovecraft said.

Thank You

FOR MANY YEARS, AS a teacher of meditation and spiritual awakening, I've wanted to serve people by opening them to radically new possibilities. The fiction I write is simply an extension of that aim. I want my novels to be fun to read and entertaining. I also want them to be educational and transformative. Most of all, I want you to finish them, put them down and feel that the world you live in after reading, is bigger, more mysterious and more wonderful than it was before.

The stories I write challenge our fundamental notions about what is real. My novels present characters who find themselves having experiences, or landing in circumstances, that force them to question everything they ever thought. What they discover, in a variety of ways, is that reality is much different than they had imagined.

Thank you for reading this novel. I deeply appreciate the time you take to read my words and I sincerely hope that you find it time well spent. If you are curious about other novels that I've written, please visit transdimensionalfiction.com and sign up to receive my newsletter.

Made in the USA
Coppell, TX
20 February 2021